# We Can Forever

## SILENT JOURNEY
### BOOK ONE

LENNA PHOENIX

WE CAN FOREVER • SILENT JOURNEY SERIES

"**H**old the door!"

I freeze, halfway to letting the front door to Knit Happens close, and look down the street. A figure runs along the sidewalk, bathed in the glow of another gorgeous Maine sunset.

Squinting, I try to figure out who it is. I don't have to wonder for long, though.

Jenny slows to a jog, breathing heavily, and grins at me. "Oh my God. I can't believe I made it in time. Please tell me. Can I get some yarn? Please, please, please?"

She clasps her hands together and bats her eyelashes at me. It's a funny and awkward sight, seeing a woman who has to be around forty putting on such a show, and all I can do is laugh.

"Yes, of course." I hold the door open for her. "I'm not saying no to one of my best customers."

"You're a lifesaver, girl. Thank you so much." Jenny scurries into the shop, and I shut the door behind us then flip the sign to closed.

"I've never heard about yarn saving lives, but there's a first time for everything."

"I'll be quick, I promise." She purses her lips and studies the rows of wool skeins. "I just need a bit to finish the scarf I'm making for Rose's teacher. It's her birthday tomorrow."

"That's sweet." I've never met her daughter, but Jenny talks about her every time she's in here. The fact that she's obviously such a good mom always warms my heart.

"Found it." Jenny selects a red skein and then watches me arrange some folding chairs in a circle. "Do you have something going on here tonight?"

"Yeah, it's a..." I wipe my hands against my jeans, suddenly nervous. "It's a meeting. A little crafting group."

A lump forms in my throat. I know there's nothing to hide, but at the same time, I'm praying she doesn't ask any more questions.

Thankfully, she turns to face the register. "That's nice. We need more things happening on this island. It's slow as molasses sometimes."

I step behind the register to ring her up. "That's the appeal, though, isn't it?"

"I guess." She fiddles with one end of the wool. "I can only imagine it's why you moved here, right? To get some peace and quiet?"

"Yeah," I agree, though there's more to it than that.

When I saw the picture of this empty storefront online, it called to me in a way nothing ever had before. Even from all the way in Portland, Oregon, I knew I'd found my shop—a place for my dreams to take flight.

"I'm so glad you came." Jenny hands me some cash. "The shop is amazing, and we all love having you here so much. I hope it's not too small-town for you. I know people can really get into everyone's business around here..."

I hand her the change, wondering why she's in such a talkative mood. She's always friendly, but it seems like nerves are running her tongue tonight.

The front door opens, and Flick enters the shop. She's still wearing her canvas work apron, and her long, dark brown hair is pulled back in a messy bun. I give her a quick wave, but since Jenny hasn't stopped to take a breath, I have no time to say hello.

"...It can get lonely here too. There are some really nice men, though. Are you single?" Jenny cocks her head at me.

The question nearly makes me lose my balance. "Am I... uh..."

Flick steps up to the counter, and I can already tell what that glint in her eyes means. Though we've only known each other for a handful of months, Flick and I were basically best friends from day one, and we can read each other like a book.

"She's single," Flick announces. "Very, very single."

When I narrow my eyes at Flick, it's half in playfulness, half in annoyance. "Thank you," I say, making my tone as dry as possible. "Would you like to add another 'very' on to that?"

She laughs. "Nah, I'm good."

Jenny raps the counter in excitement. "Excellent! I have the perfect guy for you! Oh, wait—are you into men? I should have asked first."

My cheeks warm. "Yes, I like men."

I just haven't had much to do with them in years. Not because I don't appreciate them, but because life has a way of pumping the brakes sometimes, whether we like it or not.

"Who is he?" Flick leans her elbow on the counter and turns to face Jenny, transfixed.

"Michael. My brother."

"Oh." Flick's eyebrows shoot up, but I can't tell what that means.

"He's really sweet," Jenny says.

"Handsome, too," Flick adds with a wink at me.

"Um. Okay." I lick my lips, my heart racing. This isn't at all what I was expecting tonight, and it's starting to get a little overwhelming.

"He does have a kid." Jenny studies me. "So, if that's a dealbreaker—"

"It's not." I tuck a strand of hair behind my ear. "I love kids. I don't date much, though. I'm kind of out of practice."

"Then you're perfect for him."

My belly warms. I haven't even considered dating in a while, but the thought of spending a romantic evening with a man is tempting...

"What does he look like?"

Jenny shakes her head. "I can't tell you that. Blind dates always work the best when you don't know that much about the other person. Are you free tomorrow night?"

I gulp. "Sure."

"Yes!" Jenny's arms shoot high into the air, her jacket sleeves sliding down to reveal the black floral tattoos dotting her skin. "You eat pizza, right? He'll come pick you up here at seven."

I cut my gaze to Flick, hoping she'll come through with some details. Going into situations blindfolded doesn't work well for me. It's best to have all the information I can, because that's how I manage my energy and my symptoms. I need to know the factors that will affect my day, because otherwise, things can get very bad, very fast.

"You'll love him." Jenny grabs her skein and walks backward toward the door. "I promise."

There's no chance for me to say anything else, because a second later, she's out the door. There's also no chance for me to grill Flick on Michael, because not two seconds later, the door opens again and two women enter.

"Hi." One of the women, a brunette with bright-green eyes,

looks hesitantly between me and Flick. "Is this the Chronic Pain Crafting group?"

"Yes, it is." My heart does a flip. I've been so worried that no one would show up for the first meeting, I'm in danger of crying tears of happiness.

"Oh, good." The other woman, whose straight dark-blonde hair hangs down her back, smiles at us. Her makeup is impeccable, and her nails are long and perfectly manicured.

Not only am I happy they've arrived, I'm also glad for the distraction. The thought of going on my first date in five years is enough to make me break out in hives.

"Please, have a seat." I gesture at the circle where I've placed eight folding chairs, borrowed from the church down the street.

The other three take their seats while I finish setting out the water bottles and snacks. My hands shake slightly, and I do my best to calm my nerves. Tonight is so much bigger than just meeting other women with chronic pain—although that's also something I've wanted to do for a while.

What I said to Jenny earlier about yarn never saving lives was only partly a joke. Crazy as it is, yarn did kind of save mine.

Well, knitting did, more specifically.

During those weeks following my breakup with Paul five years ago, I spent hours each day on the couch at my aunt's house, knitting and purling through all the pain and worries. Every stitch cleared my head a little more, and whenever I finished a project, I saw confirmation that, despite the challenges in life, I could still persevere and create worthwhile things.

I want to share that with others—not just in classes for all adults and kids, but also for people living with silent and chronic illnesses.

People like me.

Today, finally, is my soft launch. The first notch in my belt that will be followed by more classes and—hopefully—funding from the state to cover my store hours so I can keep doing this.

Taking a seat on one of the cold, hard chairs, I place my hands on my knees. I've prepared a script for tonight, and thank God for it. Even though I've been on Pine Island for about half a year, my haunts are still exclusively Knit Happens, my house, and the grocery store.

When it comes to people, my interactions are limited to discussions about the best kind of needles for different projects and what the fresh catch of the day is.

"Welcome, everyone." My voice catches, and I clear my throat. "Thank you for coming. I would love it if we could all introduce ourselves by saying our names, our preferred knit craft, and, if you want, your illness. I'll go first."

The silence in the room is deafening, and even though only three sets of eyes are on me, I feel as if I might buckle under the weight of them.

But then I remember why we're here tonight, what joins us all together, and strength surges through me. "I'm Hannah. I love making amigurumi, and I have fibromyalgia."

The second the last word leaves my lips, I feel a weight lift from my shoulders. I don't usually talk about my illness, but naming it in front of these people, even though two of them are strangers, is so freeing.

The other women are nodding and giving me sympathetic looks, and I can tell that I won't need to explain fibromyalgia to them. They already know about the pain, the fatigue, the having to constantly measure how much energy you have so that you don't overexert yourself and end up in the middle of a flare before you can even process what's happening.

Taking a deep breath, I let the warmth rush through me. Two minutes into this meeting and I know for a fact that starting it was a good choice.

"Hi, I'm Flick." She waves at the two women whose names we haven't gotten yet. "I have rheumatoid arthritis, and I'm a yarn dyer. I work out of my condo here on the island. My favorite knitting project? Hmm, let's see... I'll have to go with the good ole classic scarves."

We look at the brown-haired woman, who is probably about thirty and has her hands folded between her knees. "I'm Maya. I work at Hamilton Elementary. I teach art. I have lupus."

"What's your favorite knit craft?" Flick asks.

"Oh. Uh, I'm not sure. I've never done anything like this. I do nearly every other medium in my classes, but not knitting or crochet. Alexis told me about this, and I thought it sounded like fun."

"Hi. I'm Alexis," the other woman, who I guesstimate is in her midthirties, says. "I'm a remote food writer with interstitial cystitis. I knitted some socks in high school and they turned out pretty awful, so I'd love to take a second go at them."

We all chuckle, and it's as if the air in the room sparkles with opportunity and hope. It's been hard the last six years, ever since I started having the symptoms that would end up changing my life. To call these diseases we all have "invisible" is only the tip of the iceberg. Receiving a diagnosis is one step in the journey. After that comes all the other ways that society and people can overlook you, all the ways that they can diminish your experience or call you a liar—either directly or through suggestion or a certain look in their eye.

Being here, in this room with women who I know for a fact see me... It means more than I can put into words.

Before the emotion can spill out of me in the form of tears, I clap my hands together. "Right. So, I figured we could start with a sort of 'how-to' knit class tonight. If you're already comfortable with knitting, I have some designs I pulled out that you can take your pick from."

We get to work, selecting our projects and tools. The chatter in the room rises, and the next thing I know, we've moved our chairs closer together and there's never a beat of silence.

"Dessert hummus," Alexis is telling Flick, while she casts on some orange yarn. "Everyone is crazy about it now."

Flick makes a face. "Like, chocolate hummus?"

"Oh yeah. And other kinds too."

I study Maya's needles, where she's making great progress starting her first-ever scarf. "I used to teach, too," I tell her.

"Oh, really?" Her eyes light up. "Where?"

"Back in Oregon. I stopped because it got to be too much with my symptoms. I started doing tutoring online, and then—"

"You ended up here."

"Exactly," I laugh.

She gives me an appreciative look. "I'm glad you did. And I'm glad you started this group. This island is so small. I would have thought no one here but Alexis would understand what it's like, you know, living this way."

I nod. "It feels lonely sometimes."

"Yeah," she says softly, lowering her eyes.

"Hey, Maya." Flick turns to her. "You teach at Hamilton, right? Do you know Michael Greer? He has an eleven-year-old daughter. I don't remember her name..."

My heart rate picks up. So, Michael's kid is eleven?

I try to glean some information from that little nugget, but it doesn't tell me anything. I love kids but have never dated anyone with them, so I don't really have a daily look into what parenting is like.

"I know who he is." Maya puts her knitting in her lap. "He grew up on Pine Island and just moved back. I've never talked to him, though. We haven't had the autumn parent-teacher conferences yet. Katie is a great kid, though. And…" She smiles shyly. "The other teachers say that Michael is easy on the eyes."

"Hannah has a blind date with him," Flick says.

Alexis gasps, and suddenly, all the attention in the room is on me. I shrug, doing my best to keep my hands moving. I've dropped yet another stitch, though—my fifth one.

Just how attractive is Michael? What if he's out of my league? Not that I'm ugly—I mean, I don't think—but I also don't think I'm anything to write home about.

"Sorry," Flick whispers to me, as the other two start a conversation about their knitting. "I shouldn't have announced that."

"No, it's okay." I shake my head. "I'm just… I haven't been on a date in a long time."

"I know." She gives me a sympathetic look. I've told her all about Paul and how I've been too busy to date since him.

"What if it's just a mess?" I sigh. "What if—"

"If it's a mess, then you send me an SOS text, and I'll call you with some sort of yarn-based emergency that you need to attend to immediately. Like a crate of vicuña just became available and we have to go to the wholesale store and wrestle the other vendors for it. And if all goes well…that's a good thing."

"Is he really that hot?" I whisper. "How hot is he? On a scale of one to ten?"

Flick takes my knitting out of my hands. "I'm not going to answer that because I don't want you to work yourself up even more. Just know that you deserve someone hot and kind and good to you, and dating is the way to get there."

I take my knitting back from her. "Thank you."

She stares me down. "Remember how nervous you were about tonight's meeting?"

"Of course." I was barely able to sleep for weeks leading up to it.

"And look how well it's going."

I glance at Alexis and Maya, who are admiring each other's work. A smile pulls at my lips. Flick is right. I was super anxious about tonight, and despite that, everything turned out great.

So maybe tomorrow's date will be the same.

Either way, at least I'm going for it. I'm taking the plunge and getting outside my comfort zone. And if I do something embarrassing on the date and fall flat on my face, I can always come back to the shop and bury myself in a mountain of yarn skeins.

## Chapter Two

MICHAEL

"**D**ad? Dad!"

"Huh? What?" I drop the layout plans I've been poring over and spin around. "What is it? What's wrong?"

Katie frowns at me from her seat at the kitchen table. "We need help with these fractions."

Her cousin Rose sighs in frustration. "Our teacher didn't show us how to do it."

I highly doubt that's the case—more like the girls weren't paying attention. I get it, though. School wasn't exactly a walk in the park for me either, and I would rather have been playing out in the woods any day than sitting in a classroom.

"Let's take a look." Leaving the plans for the firehouse kitchen on the counter, I pull up a chair between Katie and Rose. "Do you remember the first step?"

"Uh-huh." Katie picks up her pencil and then does some math that makes zero sense.

"What's that?" I raise my eyebrow at my daughter.

"It's the first step."

I literally scratch my head. Well, shit. "That's not how I was taught to do it."

"That's because you went to school, like, forty years ago," Rose says, completely serious.

I nearly choke on air. "I'm not even forty. How is that possible?"

"He's thirty-five," Katie says, matter-of-fact.

"See, look how good you two are with numbers. You know who has an answer for this? YouTube." I pull out my phone and find a video on how to take care of fractions the modern way.

With the girls back on track, I head over to my plans again. I'm still not sure about how much I want to prioritize extra counter space, and, silly as it sounds, it's a problem that's been keeping me up at night.

This isn't just a kitchen I'm redoing. It isn't just another contracting job.

It isn't even about making a good impression as Pine Island's new fire chief.

It's more than that. This project is important in a way that wrings my heart.

Even if I don't want to think too hard about it.

The back door opens, and Jenny walks in, bag over her shoulder, knitting needles and a half-done scarf in her hands. "Hey, all."

"Hi, Mom." Rose doesn't bother looking up from her phone.

Wait. Her phone?

"Hold on." I fold my arms over my chest. "What happened to your homework?"

"We're done." Katie looks over Rose's shoulder and giggles at something on the screen.

"Hey, guess what?" Jenny knits as she stands in my kitchen.

"What?" I lean back against the counter.

"You have a date tomorrow night with Pine Island's newest shop owner."

"Uh... Excuse me?"

"You'll thank me later."

I cut my gaze to the girls. Katie has obviously overheard what my sister has said, and she's waiting for my reaction.

I clear my throat. "Jenny, I want to show you something in the...my room."

Once we're at the other end of the house, I shut the bedroom door. "What are you thinking? Bringing up a date in front of Katie?"

She makes a face. "Come on, Michael. Give her some credit. She can handle more than you think. Anyway, this town is so small and nosy, she would have heard about the date from someone else anyway."

I cross my arms again. I can't deny that, but still, there's the other part of this issue. "I didn't say I would go on the date."

"So, you don't want to do it?" The way she's eyeing me makes me feel so exposed.

Jenny has always been good at reading people. It's probably one of the reasons she's such a successful therapist. I'm forever asking her opinion on people. When she turns the talent on me, though, it's a different story.

"I..." I run my hand over my head, noticing that I need a haircut. Shit, I'm not even ready for a date.

In more ways than one.

"Hey." Her tone softens. "I know. It's been a long time. It'll be good for you, though. It'll be something new. And it's not like you have to run to the chapel and get married to anyone."

"But you want me to."

She bites her bottom lip, something she does when she's trying to hide her true feelings.

I sigh. "Okay, fine. So, who is this woman? Who did you pick?"

"I can't tell you that. Just show up at Knit Happens at seven tomorrow night, and she'll be there."

"So, she owns Knit Happens?" My sister makes a motion of zipping her lips. I can't help but shake my head and smirk.

"Wear something green. That sweater Mom gave you a couple years ago will be nice. It'll bring out the gold flecks in your eyes."

"I know how to dress," I say, though I already know I'll be taking her advice and wearing the sweater.

She ignores my attitude. "Katie can come over to our house tomorrow. We'll all have a pizza-making party, and then she can spend the night. That way, if the date goes well, you can see it through." She winks.

I groan. "Damn, Jenny, way to make it awkward."

She opens the door on a laugh. "Relax. I'm not asking for a play-by-play."

I follow her into the kitchen, where Rose already has her backpack on. "Can I have extra gaming time tonight?"

"What about your chores?" Jenny tucks some loose hair behind Rose's ear.

"I'll get them done really fast!" Rose darts out the back door.

"Remember," Jenny calls over her shoulder as she leaves as well. "Green sweater!"

The second the door closes, Katie is on me. "What was Aunt Jenny talking about? You have a date?"

"Uh..." I shift awkwardly, unsure of how to approach this.

But then I remember the promise I made to myself years ago—that I would never lie to her. The two exceptions to this pertained to Santa and the Tooth Fairy, and by five, she'd uncovered the truth about both of them.

So, I do what only makes sense. "Yes. I have a date."

There it is. I guess I'm going on a date.

Which is insane. I don't date.

Ever.

"A date with who?" She studies me intensely from behind her wire-rimmed glasses, and I remember what Jenny said about her being able to handle more than I give her credit for.

"I'm not sure. Your aunt set it up." I watch for her reaction.

"Oh." She gets the orange juice carton from the fridge and pats me on the shoulder. "Good. It's about time."

"I—it's about time?" I sputter. "Since when are you keeping track?"

Unfazed, she pours a glass of juice. "The longer you go without dating, the harder it will be. Better to rip the Band-Aid off, like you told me when I skinned my knee."

Taking her orange juice, she leaves the kitchen. A moment later, the sound of her bedroom door closing echoes through the house.

I stay planted by the counter, my head swimming. When and how did my kid get so wise?

Then again... I catch sight of the orange juice carton on the counter, lid dropped on the floor, and dribbles of juice on the stove.

She's not yet one hundred percent developed when it comes to everything.

I consider calling her back in to clean up after herself, but I need the silence and space to think, so I put the orange juice away and then start stress-cleaning the whole kitchen.

Jenny and Katie are right. It has been too long since I've been on a date.

It's not like I haven't been with other women in the eleven years since Talia and I split, but none of those weekend flings— or, sometimes, just nights—were meant to last.

Actual dating is different, a whole new ball game.

Am I ready for it? What will I even talk about with this woman? My whole life is Katie and work—first contracting, now running the fire station here.

I scrub the stovetop harder, my stress mounting. If nothing else, I can just end the date. Tell her I'm sorry and leave.

But I can't deny that I'm actually a little excited. Not just to meet someone new, but to spend an evening not having to put out little fires—both literal and metaphorical. An evening to just be *me*.

And who knows? Maybe Jenny is right, and this will be the start of something new.

# Chapter Three

## HANNAH

My phone beeps on the counter, and I yip in surprise.

Usually, the sound of a text wouldn't make me so jumpy, but today is different. Today is *the day*. I'm going on my first date in years.

The mere thought makes me dizzy. I'm trying not to spiral and fixate on all the ways tonight can go wrong, but it's hard. I don't even know this guy, and yet it feels like so much is riding on tonight.

Checking my phone, I find that the text, predictably, is from Flick.

*You should wear that black dress you crocheted. It's sexy but won't look like you're trying too hard.*

Sighing, I put down the phone. I still have to do the books, and I have no time to run back home before seven. So it's jeans and the mahogany blouse that I already have on.

At least I brought some makeup so I can touch up ahead of time.

It's not the first text Flick has sent about tonight's date.

She's been an endless well of advice, and while I appreciate it, the input is also starting to make me stressed. I know I should ask her to stop, but she's just trying to help and I don't want to hurt her feelings. That would be stressful, too, and make things awkward between us.

My phone starts ringing. Assuming it's Flick calling with some more advice, I huff and pick it up—but it's my aunt Carol.

"Hey," I answer, relief flooding me at the opportunity to speak with her.

"Hey, sweetie. How are you? How was work today?"

"Good." I take a seat on the stool behind the counter. "Things are busy."

"That's wonderful." The familiar sounds of home drift over the line, all the way from Oregon—the gentle gurgling of water as she fills the teakettle, her cat Einstein meowing for attention in the background.

It's almost enough to make me miss Portland, but not quite. As much good that happened there, there were also a lot of heavy times. In Maine, I've shed a lot of the past. People don't know me here, and, in a way, I don't know myself either. It's been easier to take off the old identity and put on a new one, that of a knitting store owner who lives in a historic cottage and keeps to herself.

"Have you made any more friends?" Carol asks.

"Actually, yeah." I bite into a smile. "You know that group I was thinking about starting? For people with chronic pain? Flick and I held the first one the other night, and two women came."

"Oh Hannah, that's lovely."

"And...I have a date. Tonight."

Silence.

"Really?" Carol asks.

"Yeah." Why did it take her so long to respond?

"With whom? Someone on the island? How did you meet him? Send me a picture. Or his Facebook. He's on Facebook, right? It's a red flag if someone isn't, you know. Or if they have more than one Facebook profile. Gail Douglas's cousin—"

"Carol," I cut in. "It's a blind date. I don't know anything about him."

"You... Oh." I can nearly feel her worry, the source of both her silence and then sudden rapid-fire interrogation.

"Don't worry. We're going somewhere public. It'll be fine."

"I know. You're a smart girl, Hannah." Another loaded silence. "Do you still have that pepper spray I gave you? Keep it on your keychain."

"I will," I say, though it's so old, it probably doesn't even work anymore. "I need to go. He'll be here soon."

"Okay. You have a good night. Love you."

"I love you too. Bye." Hanging up, I let out a long sigh.

Carol tries to hide her worry about me, but every once in a while, something pushes it to the surface and it becomes glaringly obvious. And as much as I love my aunt, the woman who raised me, the only family I have, and I crave her company... sometimes it's a bit much. I'm already nervous enough as it is, which is why it's best we continue this conversation after the date.

That way, if there's anything to worry about, we can do it in retrospect and not from a place of anxiety.

Refocusing, I pivot to the shop's books, the last task on my list for the day. After crunching the numbers, I do it a second time and get the same result. One that makes me smile.

Knit Happens is doing even better than I thought. I'm beyond breaking even. I'm actually thriving.

Not too shabby, considering many businesses fail in their first year, and others only make just enough to keep going. But look at me, living the dream.

Still grinning, I close my bookkeeping software and open my email for one last check. The message at the top of my inbox makes my stomach do a flip.

Nerves racing through me, I open the message. It's a reminder about the deadline to apply for private craft funding. I have two more weeks to get my submission together. After that, fingers crossed, maybe I'll receive the grant that will let me hire employees so that I can teach crafting classes out of the store.

I had meant to at least start my application by now, but between the store and limiting my tasks so I don't have flare-ups, I just haven't had any free time.

Quickly, I close the tab and shut my computer. I have enough to worry about tonight, and Michael will be here in less than twenty minutes.

Hurrying to the bathroom, I pull out my makeup bag and start touch-ups. My hair is a little limp, but I didn't bring anything to freshen it up so I settle on a small French braid on either side. My shoulder-length blonde hair is a little short for the look, but it ends up pretty cute.

Add some mascara and powder, and I'm starting to feel good about myself. Pulling out my nude pink lipstick, I start to apply a fresh coat, but a knock on the front door makes me freeze.

Lipstick to my mouth, I stare at myself in the mirror. He's here!

Just like that, all my nerves return. Quickly, I finish my lipstick, stow my makeup bag under the sink, and head to the front of the store.

At the sight of the man on the other side of the glass door, I freeze. Ho-lee...

"Shit," I breathe.

Based on what Maya said, I'd expected Michael to be attractive, but what's standing in front of me is a whole different level of hot. Tall and muscular, with a square jaw and thick, dark brown hair, he looks like he just walked out of a magazine.

Are people this attractive even allowed out in society? Shouldn't they be kept somewhere behind glass display cases? A man like this probably causes car accidents every time he walks down the street. Because what driver, with this in front of them, could ever be expected to keep their eyes on the road?

My whole body buzzing, I walk to the door. When he catches sight of me, his eyes widen slightly, and then...he smiles.

Genuinely smiles, like he's happy to see me.

My heart tittering, I unlock and open the door. "Hi. Michael?"

"Yes. Michael Greer." He extends his hand.

"Hannah Lewis." I slide my palm into his, and electricity crackles across my skin and up my arm as we shake.

"Hannah." He says my name like it's poetry, and the deep timbre of his voice makes it all the better. "It's a pleasure to meet you."

"You too." Realizing I'm still holding on to his hand, I swiftly drop it. "I just need to finish closing up. It should only take a few minutes. Would you like to come in?"

"Sure."

I'm intensely aware of his close presence as he follows me into the shop. "Make yourself comfortable."

He lingers by the wall. "That's a lot of yarn by the radiator. That could be a fire hazard."

"O...kay." I grab my purse, not sure how to react to such a random comment.

His face turns pink. "Sorry. Bad habit. I'm a firefighter."

"You are?" So then maybe he walked out of a calendar rather than off a magazine cover.

"I'm the fire chief here." He stuffs his hands into his pockets, and I realize for the first time that he's probably as nervous as I am.

Which, ironically, makes me less nervous.

"That's cool. Stopping fires is important."

Oh God. Did I really just say that? I sound like a second grader presenting her report on what firefighters do.

He chuckles. "I think so."

My face hot, I turn away from him, using the excuse of switching off most of the lights. "Ready to go?"

"Absolutely."

He holds the door open for me, and we head out into the chilled dusk. Understanding that we're both coming from the same place—sheer nervousness—is helping me breathe easier, even despite the awkward comment I just made about his job. We might be strangers, but at least we have one thing in common.

"Jenny says we should have pizza." Michael starts slowly walking down the sidewalk. "Apparently it's the perfect first-date meal."

"Oh, is it now?" I laugh.

"Yeah," he chuckles.

"Jenny has a lot of opinions, doesn't she?"

"That's one way to put it." He grins down at me, and I'm struck by how tall he is, how broad his shoulders are. I'm feeling things I haven't felt in years, and we've known each other all of five minutes.

"Michael!" A man with thinning gray hair approaches. "Heard you're picking up your dad's old project, renovating the firehouse kitchen."

"Er, uh, yes. I am." Michael stiffens slightly.

"Your dad sure would have liked to see those windows replaced."

Michael nods. "I might get to them. There are some other priorities first."

The man shakes his head. "Your dad knew what he was talking about."

Michael's jaw tightens, but he smiles through it. "Thanks, Lou. I'll keep that in mind. See you later."

We start walking again, but we haven't gone even a few steps before Mrs. Krohn comes out the front door of her realty office. "Well, hey there! How are the renovations going on the firehouse?"

It's like that for the rest of the two-block walk to Get Stuffed. It seems everyone in town has heard about Michael renovating the firehouse kitchen. Everyone but me, that is.

Michael is kind to all of them, but underneath his soft voice and smile I can sense the tension. I don't know whether anyone else can see it, but he's eager to finish each conversation.

And I would really like my date to myself.

"People are really curious about what you're doing," I comment as we finally reach the pizza place.

He sighs. "That's one way to put it. I'm sorry."

I shake my head. "It's okay. Don't be."

He holds his arm outstretched toward the door. "Shall we?"

It's such a romantic, formal gesture for such a casual setting, that I have to laugh.

"What?" He asks.

"Nothing. I just... I like that we did this. I was nervous."

He drops his arm. "We haven't even started dinner yet."

My face warms. Oh no. Did I just put my foot in my mouth? Do I look too eager?

"I—" I try to recover, but Michael is going on.

"But I'm glad, too." His bright hazel eyes drink me in.

A giddiness wells in my chest, and I accept his offer to hold the door open for me. As we walk into the restaurant, I feel the kind of excitement that I haven't had since I decided to open Knit Happens.

This date isn't at all what I expected, but maybe it's exactly what I need.

Chapter Four

MICHAEL

Hannah walks in front of me as we make our way through Get Stuffed and to a table in the back, and I take the opportunity to smile as big as I feel like.

I had my reservations about tonight, but the moment I set my eyes on her, I was floored. I'm not even sure what I noticed first—her big blue eyes, the freckles splashed across her button nose, or her pink, full lips. They're all perfect.

And I feel like one very lucky man.

"Hey, Michael." Emmy Jane, one of the waitresses, approaches us before we've even taken a seat.

"Hi, Emmy Jane. How are you?"

She ignores the question and splits a smile between Hannah and me. "It's so good to have you both in. We have some appetizers here, on the house."

She unloads her tray, placing jalapeño poppers, breadsticks, and the house salad on the table. "What can I get you to drink?"

"Oh." Hannah looks up at her. "Thank you. I doubt we can eat all this..."

"Don't worry about it. Christine just wanted to make sure

you have whatever you want for your special night. On the house," she repeats.

Through the kitchen window, Christine, whose husband volunteers part time at the fire station, waves at me. I wave back, embarrassed that we have about the same amount of privacy in here as we did on the street.

"I'll take water," I tell Emmy Jane.

"Same," Hannah says, and Emmy Jane bustles off with a nod.

"You know everyone." Hannah rests her clasped hands on the table.

"More like everyone knows me." I hesitate. "I'm sorry. We can go somewhere more—"

"No, it's okay. Small town. I get it." She fiddles with her fork. "So, you're renovating the fire station?"

"Not the whole thing." I fold my arms on the table, happy to at least have something to talk about. "Just the kitchen. I was a contractor before I moved back here and took over my dad's job."

"As fire chief. After he retired?"

"After he...died."

Her lips part in surprise. "Oh. I'm sorry."

"Thank you." A lump forms in my throat, and I have to work to swallow it down. "The last project he had going before he passed was this. He wanted to revamp the whole kitchen, which is pretty old. I guess people have opinions about it."

"When did he pass?"

"Last year. He, uh... We had a big fight the last time we saw each other. He disagreed with my parenting choices. Thought I should move back to Pine Island so Katie could be around family."

I have no clue why I'm opening up like this. Maybe it's because I know she'll eventually hear this story from someone else, or maybe it's because I feel at ease around her and I want to speak what's constantly on my mind.

"We never got the chance to make up," I add.

My last word hangs in the air. I wish there were more to add, but that's it. That's the end of the story.

Resolutions are for books and movies. When you get them in real life, it's a bonus, not a guarantee.

I clear my throat, suddenly uncomfortable. This topic isn't exactly first-date material, and I don't want to bring down the mood.

"What brought you to Pine Island?" I ask. "Your shop?"

"Exactly." Her whole demeanor changes. Her face becomes brighter, and she sits straighter. "I'm from Oregon. Portland. I was working from home, teaching online, and I saw the storefront when I was searching for some examples for a course, and... I can't explain it. I just fell in love with what I saw. It was so right."

"So you came and checked it out, and that was that?"

"Not exactly," she laughs. "My aunt checked it out for me, and I bought it on the spot."

I cock my head. "You were willing to take that chance without looking at the place yourself or visiting the island?"

"Um. Well..." She bites her bottom lip. "I wasn't feeling well, and we knew the property would go fast."

Emmy Jane arrives out of nowhere and places our drinks on the table. "Two waters. Now, what can I get you for dinner?"

We decide on a pizza to share, and as soon as Emmy Jane leaves, Hannah turns back to me. "Tell me about your daughter."

I would like to hear more about her, actually, but the fact that she seems to genuinely want to know about Katie is wonderful. One of the reasons I've put off dating is that I worry what people will think of me having a kid, and that's just the start of it. From what I've learned from other people, all sorts of complications come into place when you date with children involved.

"Katie is eleven." Just speaking about her makes me feel lighter. "She's smart, really...intuitive. She gets that from her aunt Jenny, I guess. She liked that I was going on a date tonight. Basically told me that it's time to get back out there."

Hannah laughs. "Wow. She's not afraid to speak her mind."

"Tell me about it," I chuckle.

"How long has it been?"

I press my tongue against my front teeth, not sure I want to admit the truth. "Would you think less of me if I said years?"

"Nope." She seems completely unfazed. "Not if you don't think less of me if I say the same thing."

"Really? You haven't been on a date in years?"

I find that hard to believe. A woman this beautiful must have men constantly throwing themselves at her. Did she leave a relationship recently? Is that why she hasn't been dating?

"I'm going to need an explanation for that." I scoot my chair farther into the table, only because it gets me a couple inches closer to her.

She shrugs. "Life just kind of gets in the way. I'm sure you know about that."

I snort. "Boy, do I ever."

She selects a fried jalapeño, and I have to work not to stare while she eats it. "What kind of contracting jobs did you have before?"

"We were in Seattle, and it was all kinds. Mostly businesses. Shops. Government buildings."

"That sounds like a lot of responsibility."

"Not as much as being fire chief here. The expectations are...different."

"Oh yeah?" She cocks her head, her voice dropping. "Tell me more."

I know she's not trying to sound sultry, but the low vibrations of her voice send a shiver through me. I can't help but imagine how soft her skin must be, what she smells like up close, my face buried in her hair...

My phone buzzes in my pocket, making me jump. "I'm sorry. I should check this."

"Of course."

I pull out the phone to see that it's the station. I have to work to suppress a sigh. "I'll call them back in a minute."

But then I get a text from one of the volunteers. *Car wreck on the bridge. Could use you.*

Stuffing the phone back into my pocket, I give Hannah an apologetic look. "I'm so sorry. The crew needs me."

I'm both relieved and sad over the disappointment that flashes across her face. I hate to bail on her, but it's also nice that she wants me here.

"It's understandable." She offers up a warm smile. "Duty calls."

I gesture for Emmy Jane to bring the check, and as I hand her some cash, I turn back to Hannah. "I would love a rain check. Can I get your number?"

The second before she answers feels like a hundred years. I can't breathe. Can't think.

Finally, she smiles. "Of course."

"I have a pen." Emmy Jane, who I didn't know was still here —but of course she is; isn't everyone in this town always around?—drops the pen on the table.

After writing her number on a napkin, Hannah stands to see me off. It's that part of the evening when I have no clue what to do, and when she moves in for a quick hug, I peck her on the cheek.

I was right. Her skin *is* incredibly soft. Like satin. And she smells like fresh rain and a field of lavender, which, starting now, are my two new favorite scents.

Pulling myself together, I step back. "Thank you. I'm sorry again. I'll call you."

She nods. "I'd like that. Now go do your thing."

Even though I want to stay right by her side, I will myself to walk out of the restaurant and to my truck, parked just down the street. With each step, my heart becomes a little lighter.

Since I've moved back to Pine Island, life has been good, but it's also felt like it's missing something. Hell, the last eleven years have felt that way. I love being a dad, but I've always longed for something additional... Something I never fully let myself crave.

Tonight, the tide is changing. I feel it in the air.

Good things are on their way.

## Chapter Five

### HANNAH

Pulling into a parking spot at the local elementary school, I take a moment to check my reflection in the rearview mirror. To my surprise, my pulse is racing.

Though I love teaching, it's been years since I've actually set foot in a classroom. The demands of an in-person teaching job are heavy enough, but add fibromyalgia flare-ups to the mix, and it doesn't end well.

So, I left my art classes at the high school. Just like I had to leave so much in life behind.

Yet now, here I am. About to teach a knitting class to kids, courtesy of Maya. While I once thought I'd left this passion behind for good, it turns out I only put it on pause.

Realizing that washes away any lingering anxiety. This is what I'm meant to be doing, where I'm meant to be.

Grabbing my purse and bag of things for the class, I leave the car and stride across the parking lot.

It feels weird to have left the shop so early in the afternoon, but Flick more than has it under control. Besides, I could use the distraction. I've already finished everything on my to-do list for the next two weeks, and I even completed two of the knitting projects I abandoned months ago.

It would probably be wise to slow down, just to prevent a flare-up, but I've been on hyperdrive the last few days. Ever since that date with Michael, he's been on my mind nonstop.

We've texted a few times, but other than that, it's been radio silence. Flick has assured me this is normal—he probably doesn't want to come on too strong, and he might be busy with work and his daughter.

Even though she's right, I can't stop myself from checking my phone every five minutes. I feel like a teenager with a crush.

It's thrilling. But terrifying too.

What if this whole thing crashes and burns? What if...

Shaking off the worries, I sign in at the front office. No more catastrophizing. Not for now anyway. It's time to bring my A game.

After locating the classroom, I knock on the door and wait. Maya appears in the window, wearing a bright smile and a knit sweater over a sundress.

"Hi!" She opens the door for me to enter. "Class, this is our knitting teacher, Miss Hannah."

The kids are gathered around the room, doing various things, but they all stop and turn to me. I smile and wave at them all, wondering which one of them is Katie—who Maya informed me would be in this class.

"Hi, everyone." I lift the bag I'm carrying. "I brought lots of yarn to choose from. Today, we're going to learn how to cast on, and then we'll start scarves. How does that sound?"

The responses vary from completely ignoring me to clapping in excitement, which is to be expected. Putting the bag on a table, I start unpacking the skeins and needles.

"Thank you for this," I whisper to Maya.

"Of course. I'm so glad you could come."

When I mentioned to her that I need experience teaching crafting to add to my funding application, she jumped in with the offer to have me come to one of her classes. Luckily, the school cleared me as a volunteer almost immediately.

With the skeins set out, I turn back to the class. "Let's start by picking out the color that you'll use for your scarf."

The kids advance on the table, and I scan their name tags. Right away, I find Katie. Her skin is darker than Michael's, but she has the same wide mouth and intelligent eyes. The girl next to her, Rose, has a name tag with the same last name.

Katie's cousin? And Jenny's daughter?

Seeing them makes me nervous all over again. Have they heard about my date with Michael? Has he mentioned me to them at all?

Everyone takes a skein, and then we all gather on the cushions in the back corner of the room.

"To start off, you want to figure out how thick you want your scarf to be." I demonstrate, then show them how to cast on stitches.

Predictably, some of the kids catch on right away, while others need to see me do it over and over again. It's always like this when people first start knitting, and the jubilant look on their faces when they finally get it right never gets old.

Maya and I go around the cushions helping the students out, and when I reach Katie and Rose, I do my best to act like a normal person.

"Hi, girls. How's it going?" I crouch next to them.

Katie holds up her skein. "We can't decide if this is lavender or—"

"Twilight," Rose inserts. "It should be called twilight."

I bite the inside of my cheek so that I don't laugh. "I don't remember what the manufacturer calls that color, but I suppose you can name it anything you want. How is casting on going?"

They show me their needles, where they each have successful rows of stitches.

"Beautiful," I comment, handing Rose's project back to her.

Out of the corner of my eye, I catch Katie watching me with her head cocked. When I turn to her, though, she quickly looks down.

Does she know who I am? That I went on a date with her father?

If so, what does she think of that? Does it make her curious about me? Irritated by my presence? It's hard to put myself in her shoes. I never knew my father and Carol never married, so I don't even have an uncle.

"Keep up the good work," I force out before moving on to the next kid.

We don't interact anymore the rest of class, and once our time is up, I grab my now-empty bag and give Maya a hug.

"This was great." Maya releases me. "What are you doing tomorrow night? Would you like to get a drink?"

Warmth spreads through my chest. All these months, I've pretty much had one friend on Pine Island. One friend, no classes to teach, and no hot dates.

And now look at how my life is blossoming.

"I would love to," I tell her. "I'll text you later."

With a final goodbye to the class, I head out. My steps are perky, a song flowing from my lips. Sliding behind the wheel of my car, I put it in reverse and back out of the parking spot.

I have so much going for me, it feels like nothing could ever go wrong again. I almost don't even care if Michael ever calls for a second date. There's so much—

The piercing noise of metal on metal fills the air, and my car bumps to a halt. I've backed up right into a pickup truck.

In the blink of an eye, my luck has turned upside down.

"Oh my God," I gasp.

I turn around in my seat, waiting for the furious parent or teacher to emerge and yell at me. The man who gets out, though, looks oddly familiar.

I blink. Blink again.

It's *Michael*.

My jaw drops. Seriously?

I'm still trying to decide whether this makes the situation better or worse by the time he reaches my car door. My face burning, I roll down the window.

"Hello," I squeak out.

Surprise flashes across his face, but a second later, he's grinning. "What do you know?"

"I'm sorry." I cringe, wanting to dig a hole and crawl into it. According to everything I've learned online, I'm supposed to be playing hard to get right now—and driving into a man's vehicle is the opposite.

"How are you?" He bends forward so we're face-to-face.

I've just backed into his truck, and this is what he starts with? "I'm...good. How are you?"

"Better now."

I have to laugh. "I just hit your truck."

"Eh. She'll be fine. Your car, on the other hand..."

"Maybe my plan will cover it." I scramble for my insurance card, afraid to even know what he sees back there.

"You're leaving your class here, right? Katie told me about it. What are you doing now? Are you busy?"

I stop digging through my purse. "Um, no. My friend is at the store covering for me. I was going to go home and rest."

I swallow hard, wanting to tell him why I need to rest before I'm even tired but finding that explaining this requires Herculean strength.

"Hmm." He scratches his chin. "How about I take you to

my friend's auto shop. He owes me a favor. I can have him buff off the scratch on your bumper."

"That's not necessary. It was my fault, and—"

"I want to do it. I can text Jenny and have her pick up Katie and her cousin." His eyes bore into mine, and I lose strength in each muscle, including my tongue.

"O-okay," I stammer. "Thanks."

"Perfect." There's that smile again. The one that's so blinding it puts the sun to shame. When he turns it on me, I would probably do just about anything he asked.

"Perfect," I repeat, because my brain is mush and I can't think of anything original to say.

"I'll lead the way." He strides to his truck, and I follow him away from school and to the bridge that connects the mainland to Pine Island.

What at first seemed like a wrench thrown into an amazing week is turning into another blessing. The universe seems to want Michael and me to be together.

For the first time in a long while, every area of my life is looking up. I don't even feel like I'm waiting for the next shoe to drop.

Grinning like crazy, I leave my window down and catch a fresh breeze, not minding the chill. It really feels like nothing could hurt me right now anyway—and, perhaps, ever again.

# Chapter Six

## MICHAEL

"**D**o you have an hour and a half to wait?" Nathan wipes oil from his hands and looks between Hannah and me. "You could go hang out at the coffee shop for a bit."

I have to check my laugh. He's bluffing. It's the slowest part of the day; he's always talking about how he finishes the dropped-off cars in the morning and then doesn't get another rush until the islanders get off work around five.

"Do we?" Hannah turns to me.

Out of the corner of my eye, I see Nathan grin. My suspicions are confirmed—my buddy is trying to set me up.

I'll have to buy him a drink next time we go out.

I've been waiting for the perfect opportunity to ask Hannah out for a do-over, but I've been swamped with work and Katie. The fact that we bumped into each other today—literally—is perfect. And since Jenny has the girls, I can steal away for a little while.

"I do," I say. "Does that work for you?"

"Um." She adjusts her glasses and shifts her weight.

That's right. She had said she planned on going home and resting. Is she not feeling well?

"No pressure," I tell her. "I can drive you home, if you like, and then bring the car to you once it's done."

"No, don't do that." She touches my upper arm, then seems to realize what she's doing and pulls back, her face pink. "You're both doing so much for me already. I can wait, and coffee sounds good."

My stomach swoops with excitement. I meant what I said about driving her home, but I sure am glad she declined the offer. There's nothing I would rather do more right now than cozy up with her somewhere.

We head out of the garage, Nathan winking at me behind Hannah's back, and across the street to Tall Order. The afternoon sun kisses our faces, and dried leaves blow down the street. Hannah casts a shy look my way, and I grin back at her.

"After you." I open the door to the coffee shop and bakery, the delicious smells of fresh bread and roasting beans wafting out of it.

About half of the seats are taken, most of them by Pine Island's retired population and people working remotely on their laptops. The best spot is available, though, and I lead Hannah to the little table next to the fireplace.

A few logs crackle in the hearth, creating a cozy ambiance. Hannah takes off her jacket and slips into a seat.

"It's so cute in here," she comments, looking around at the plants and macramé art.

"You've never been in?" That's hard to believe.

"A few times. I never stayed, though. I just grabbed a drink and left. Plus, I don't really drink coffee."

"In that case, I feel like an idiot bringing you here."

"No!" She laughs, her face lighting up. "I would go anywhere with you."

Her eyebrows rise in shock, and she bites her lip. Obviously, that last part just slipped out, but I don't mind it at all.

"I like hearing that." I let my gaze linger on hers for a moment longer, feeling confident in a new way—a way that has nothing to do with piecing together a deck or putting out a vehicle fire in record time.

Hannah makes me feel like a man who is important in other ways. Ways that I ache to explore.

Licking my lips, I push those thoughts away for the time being. "If you don't drink coffee, how about a hot chocolate?"

"Sounds perfect. Thank you." The blush is fading from her face, but the way that she fusses with her clothes suggests she's still embarrassed. I want to tell her not to be, that everything she does and says is undeniably cute, even if she feels like she's being awkward. I have to hold back, though, yet again. I'm all too aware that if I say too much, especially about delicate things, I could scare her away.

I need to keep doing my best playing it cool.

Whatever the hell that means.

Basically, I'm making this whole thing up as I go, hoping that I'm at least doing some things right and leaving a positive impression on her.

"Be right back," I say, eager to stop thinking and just do something. I always was better with my hands.

At the counter, it's the same deal it always is when I go out in town. Cade Rignola, one of my firefighters, skips back a few spots in line to talk to me.

"Is that who you were on a date with the other day?" He nods subtly at Hannah.

"Oh, mind your own business, Cade," Summer, who owns Tall Order, says from behind the espresso machine. "Or you aren't getting that extra chocolate on top of your cappuccino."

"Hey, I'm asking what everyone wants to know." Cade raises his hands in surrender.

"How was your shift?" I ask Cade, eager to talk about something that isn't my personal life.

He gives me the general rundown as I place my order and wait. By the time I have a hot chocolate and an americano in hand, though, I'm eager to head back to Hannah and what precious time we have together.

"See you later," I tell Cade, walking back to the table as fast as I can without looking frantic.

"Thank you." Hannah takes a sip from the huge mug. A fleck of whipped cream lingers on her lips, and she dots it away with a napkin.

Heat rolls through me like a thundercloud across a summer prairie. Good God, what is wrong with me? We've barely touched, and yet I feel like a complete horndog around this woman.

"Was your class everything you wanted it to be?" I ask, half because I want to know and half because I need to distract myself from...*other* thoughts.

She beams. "It was amazing. I met Katie and Rose."

"Oh yeah?" My pulse picks up, worry threading through me. They're both polite and I'm not too worried about their behavior around adults, but this is Hannah. Someone special.

"They're really nice girls."

I sigh a little in relief. "They didn't ask you about our date, did they?"

Under the table, my knee brushes hers the slightest bit. A tingle rushes through my leg, but I pull back, not wanting her to think I'm making a move this soon.

"They're about the only people from this island who haven't asked," she laughs. If she even felt my knee touch hers, she's either playing it off well or doesn't care.

My hope is that she's just as affected by it as me.

"What did you work on with them?" I ask, trying my best to keep my mind on her class with the girls and not on...other things.

"We're doing scarves, but today was all about figuring out which yarn type is best for your project and casting on."

"Ah." I nod.

Hannah cocks an eyebrow. "You don't know what I'm talking about, do you?"

"Not one bit."

We both burst into laughter, and she shakes her head. "I can teach you sometime, if you like."

"I would love that."

She studies me over her mug. "Really?"

"Absolutely. It's been too long since I learned something new. I wish I could teach you something in return, though."

"I'm sure you know how to fix all sorts of things. I could use a lesson or two in taking care of leaky faucets and loose door hinges."

"Those things are a piece of cake. I can show you anytime."

The thought of getting a look at her house is thrilling. It's probably cozy and decorated in warm colors, just like her shop. And I wouldn't be surprised if she has a little garden behind it or some herbs in the kitchen window. She seems like she has a green thumb.

My phone beeps with a text, and I pull it out to see it's Nathan.

"Your car is ready," I announce, my stomach sinking. How did an hour fly by so fast?

"Oh." She sounds just as surprised as I am. "That was quick."

"Way too quick." Pocketing my phone, I study her—a long gaze that she blushes under.

"How about a redo of that first date?" I ask.

"I thought this was a redo."

"Then a second redo."

"Sure," she laughs. "I'd really like that."

"Awesome." I stand and lead her out of the coffee shop. As we walk onto the street, I feel multiple eyes on us, but for the first time in quite a while, I really don't care.

Let them stare. My eyes are busy too—but only for one person.

# Chapter Seven

HANNAH

"Here you go. Good as new." Nathan pats my car's bumper, which shines like it just came off the lot.

"Thank you so much. I really appreciate it. Especially after I was the one who caused the accident." I glance at Michael, still feeling like a total doofus for backing into him.

But he doesn't even blink. "It's no big deal."

"And maybe it was meant to be," Nathan adds. "I need to, ah, make a call. See you later. Nice to meet you, Hannah."

He slips into the shop's office before I can respond, and Michael and I are left alone next to my car.

From the other side of the office window, Nathan peeks at us. The second he sees me noticing, he quickly turns away.

"It doesn't look like he's making a call," I comment with a smile.

"Yeah." Michael rubs the back of his neck. "Sorry."

"I don't mind," I chuckle. "I like him. It was really nice of him to take care of my scratch."

"What are you doing tomorrow night?" Michael stuffs his hands into his jeans pockets. In the garage, his cologne is easier to pick up, and the woodsy scent has butterflies flitting through my stomach.

"I'm having drinks with a friend. Maya. The art teacher at school."

"What about the night after that?"

"Hopefully, going out with you."

The response is my attempt at confidence, but the moment the words slip out, I want to snatch them back, they're that cringey.

Michael doesn't seem to agree, though. He chuckles and takes a step closer to me. "That's what I wanted to hear."

My breathing starts to speed up. He's so close, only a foot away, the flecks of amber in his eyes shining under the shop's lights.

What will I do if he takes one more step forward and closes the distance between us? It's been so long since I've kissed someone, but I'm craving—no, aching—to be touched by this man.

"I'll call you." He steps away, and it's like my heart is torn in half.

Somehow, I manage to find my tongue. "Okay. Thank you. And thank you again for this." I gesture at my car.

"It's my pleasure." He purrs more than says the words, and my belly squirms with excitement.

Too soon, he's out of the garage, leaving me weak in the knees and hot all over.

Climbing in my car, I sigh in satisfaction. Things are going so well. Almost too well.

I shake off the almost automatic response to turn to worry. Just because life is great doesn't mean that it's about to take a nose dive. I don't owe some crazy karmic debt.

Picking up my phone, I open the text from Aunt Carol that I've been meaning to reply to all afternoon. She's asking about my date the other night.

It was great, I text her back. Oh! And I'm teaching classes at the elementary school now. My first one was today. How did your HOA meeting go?

I'm putting down the phone, about to drive to Flick's place, when it starts ringing.

"Hey," I say, answering my aunt's call.

"You're teaching at the elementary school? Is there even one on Pine Island?" she asks, jumping right into the conversation.

"It's at the closest one. On the mainland."

"Oh. Isn't that a bit much, sweetie?"

I frown over my steering wheel. "No. Why would it be too much? What do you mean?"

"I'm just concerned about your health, Hannah. Your shop is still new, and I know that takes a lot of work to run. And you have all these other side projects going on."

"What other side projects?" I laugh, trying my hardest to keep my annoyance at bay.

"Teaching at the elementary school. Your grant application. Your new meetup group—which is great. I absolutely think you should keep doing that."

"The grant application doesn't even take up that much time." That's not entirely true. It is taking hours, but it's also something that I both need and want to do.

"I don't want you to have a bad flare. That's all."

Closing my eyes, I drop my head back against the headrest. I get where she's coming from, and if she doesn't worry about me, who will? Carol is more than my aunt; she's my adoptive parent, the woman who raised me after my mom died when I was eight. She's been with me through it all, including the manifestation of mystery symptoms and the long, trying hunt for a diagnosis.

She knows as well as I do that if I push too hard, my health will be the price to pay.

What she doesn't know as well as I do are my limits. I'm doing fine right now.

There's really no way to convince her of this, though. There never is. So I say what needs to be said in the moment.

"I'll pace myself. I'll slow down."

"Thank you." She sighs in relief, and the conversation turns to other things as I drive to Flick's condo. She's closed up the shop by now, and we're due for our weekly "stitch and bitch," as we lovingly call it.

"Tell Einstein I said hi," I say to my aunt as I turn into Flick's neighborhood. "And give him a scratch on the belly for me."

We hang up, and it's a good thing I know the drive to Flick's condo like the back of my hand, because I was thoroughly distracted on the way over here, the in-between moments of my phone call full of thoughts of Michael. The things that he incites in me are crazy. I feel like a teen crushing on a pop star, and it's a little scary just how much I'm thinking about him.

I know I shouldn't dwell on it; I should just live in the moment and be open to whatever comes next. It's hard not to hope, though—and it's hard not to worry.

I would love to find a man to settle down with, but after my last attempt at love...

My stomach sours at the mere thought of Paul. Luckily, I've arrived at Flick's condo. It's time to have fun, enjoy the evening, and leave the past in the past where it belongs.

At least, that's what I want to do. Sometimes, leaving what's done is hard. Especially if it holds lessons that you can protect yourself with.

Turning into the parking lot, I find a spot in front of the walkway to Flick's door. That's a good thing about this condominium complex—there are only a small number of units, and you can usually park close. The outside always looks nice too, well-maintained with touches of the owners' personalities on their small front porches. Unlike a lot of the homes around here. Several are in need of repair in some way—a fresh coat of paint, a fence replaced—though the overall feel of Pine Island is still charming.

I wonder what Michael's house looks like. Since he's a contractor, everything is probably new and spotless-looking. There are likely fresh boards on the porch, window screens with no holes, and his bedroom...

A delicious shiver runs through me. I don't even know what his bedroom looks like, but I imagine a huge bed with a soft comforter, him sleeping in it shirtless, his hair sticking up from rolling around all night. The window cracked open, his boxers hanging loosely around his hips...

Flick's front door opens, and I jump. "Oh!"

She frowns. "You okay? What is it?"

"Nothing, I, uh..." When did I knock on the door? Was I really that distracted? "I had kind of a weird afternoon."

"Uh-oh. Did the class not go well?"

"No, that's not it. The class was great." I walk past her and hang my purse on one of the hooks by the door.

As we settle into her living room, I recount everything that happened from when I backed into Michael's truck to when we parted ways at the auto shop.

"Destiny is bringing you two together!" She claps her hands in joy. "Let's celebrate with my new tea."

Bouncing off the couch, she goes to the kitchen. The familiar sounds of her filling a teakettle and getting mugs down drift back into the living room.

I raise my voice so she can hear me. "I don't know if it's destiny, but it is nice. What do you know about him?"

"Really, not much," she calls out. "That he grew up here, left for years, came back within the last year."

"Does Katie's mom live around here?"

"I don't know. I doubt it. Katie wasn't born here."

I frown. Her mom isn't here? That's interesting, but not strange, I guess. Maybe her mom's job keeps her in Seattle, and Katie splits the year between her parents.

Flick pops her head into the living room. "Do you want honey?"

"What kind of tea is it?"

She grins. "It's my new marijuana tea infusion."

I gasp. "Yes, please. I want a card! I love that you were able to get that."

"What about your new doctor?" she calls out as she returns to her busywork. "Are you going to ask her for one?"

"She said she can get me one. I just have to wait until our next appointment."

She enters the living room with a tray laden with a teapot, two mugs, and a little honey bear. Setting it on the coffee table, she pours us each a generous amount. The woody smell fills the room, and I take a slow, careful first sip. A rich, grounding flavor slides across my tongue, and I'm in a better mood just tasting it.

I'm fortunate to have found my newest doctor, though it wasn't luck that brought me to her. After the last two doctors I tried out in Maine—the first who didn't believe fibromyalgia is real and the second who would only give me NSAIDs for my pain, despite them wrecking my stomach—I finally heard about this third one from a Knit Happens customer.

So far, it's been good. Being validated is enough to bring me to tears, and the medical marijuana card she's getting me will be a godsend.

"I'm so glad you found her." Flick settles cross-legged on the couch. "She sounds amazing."

"Anyone is better than Doctor What's-His-Face."

She snorts. "For sure."

It was at Doctor What's-His-Face's office that Flick and I met. The man turned out to be a jerk, but by the time I left the waiting room, I had Flick's number, and the rest is history.

If nothing else, I suspect I was meant to come to Pine Island to meet Flick. I've never had someone get me the way she does, and not just when it comes to a love of all things yarn and what it means to live with chronic pain. She understands my ambition, my need to never settle for a life of struggle, to always find ways to make every day better.

Plus, she's the one who encouraged me to start the Chronic Pain Crafters group. If it weren't for her, we would never have connected with Maya and Alexis, and I wouldn't be teaching at the elementary school.

"To you." I raise my mug.

Her eyebrows rise. "Why me?"

"Because you're the best friend anyone could have."

"Aw, stop." She pokes my knee. "That's not possible, because you're the best friend anyone could have."

I chuckle into my tea. "How about we tie for the title?"

"I like that." She winks. "Hey, so is there anything in particular you want me to look for at the yarn conference?"

"Yes!" I add more honey to my tea. "What's most important is finding out what the expected trends are for next year."

"Got it." She nods, all business.

"Thank you for going for me." I sigh. "If I had someone to watch the store—"

"Maybe next year you will, and then we both can go."

"That would be nice." My gaze drifts to the living room window, where the pine trees at the edge of the yard drift slightly in the wind.

If I hurry up and submit that application for funding, then yes, maybe I will have someone to cover for me next year, even if

Knit Happens still isn't making enough to hire a full-time employee.

"Wow, can you imagine life one year from now?" Flick drops her head back and gazes at the ceiling. "Maybe you and Michael will be married."

"Oh my God, Flick!" My face is flaming, but I'm also laughing. "Come on. We've been on one date."

"One point five. Today was a half date."

"That doesn't mean we're getting married." I roll my eyes, and she playfully jabs me with her elbow.

What Flick's suggesting is nothing but a fantasy...right now. Of course I would love to settle down with someone, especially a man as handsome and confident as Michael.

But will it be him?

I have no way of knowing. Although I do everything I can to make each day special, when it comes down to it, I'm just a passenger on this crazy ride called life. Even though there have been ups and downs—and more downs than ups the last five years—it genuinely seems that things are getting better.

So, who knows? Maybe one year from now, I'll be in a place that's even better than I ever could have imagined.

And maybe there will be a hunky guy by my side.

A hunky, hazel-eyed fire chief guy.

# Chapter Eight

"Hey!"

I freeze, about to unlock my truck, and turn toward the familiar voice. Nathan jogs along the sidewalk with a huge grin on his face.

"You're going to leave without thanking me?" He claps me on the shoulder.

"Thank you. I really appreciate you taking care of Hannah's bumper."

He guffaws. "No, man. I'm talking about setting the two of you up. Sending you out on a coffee date."

"Thank you for that too." I lean against my truck and cross my ankles. "Though, I hate to break it to you—we already went on one date."

"You did? How the hell didn't I hear about this?"

I shrug. "I guess you don't listen much to island gossip."

"Huh. Remind me not to change that." He steps off the curb as a woman with a baby stroller goes by. "So, how did it go?"

I cringe. "I had to leave early. Got a call from the station. We are going out again, though."

Just saying it makes something flutter through my chest. It's such a weird sensation, but not unwelcome—just something I'm unused to.

"Eh. She must not hold it against you if she said yes to another date. So, where are you taking her? I have some ideas."

"Dude." I run my hands through my hair. "You sound like Jenny."

"I'm just looking out for you. You need to get back out there, or else you'll turn into one of those weird guys who doesn't know how to talk to women."

"Okay, now you sound like Katie. She basically said the same thing, except in a kinder way."

"The kid is smart."

"What about you?" I jut my chin at him.

"What about me?"

"You know what," I volley back, not letting him get off that easily. "Have you gone on any dates lately?"

He makes a face. "I'm busy. I've got my shop, and I have... my cat." He gazes into the distance, as if considering what he just said, and huffs a laugh. "That sounds pretty lame, doesn't it?"

"Only a little," I chuckle. "Are you sure you aren't making excuses?"

"Trust me, I've been looking. On every app." He pulls out his phone and shows me that he has at least four dating apps installed.

"So you're on the apps, but you aren't going on any dates?"

He stuffs his phone back into his pocket. "We're supposed to be talking about you, not me."

"Nice dodge." I don't try to hide my smirk. "But seriously, maybe you should do more than swipe left. You're a great guy."

"Yeah, that's what they all say," he retorts, rolling his eyes but looking a bit pleased. "You need to worry about yourself and the lovely lady who's agreed to another date."

"Oh, now the advice is back on me. Hypocrite." I laugh, nudging him with my elbow.

"Well, someone has to help you navigate your way in the dating world. Might as well be the resident 'great guy,'"

"Okay, so what advice do you have for me?" I'm giving him a hard time, but I'm also being serious. It's been years since I've dated, and I'm so out of practice it's embarrassing.

"Well," he begins slowly, tapping on his chin as he formulates his TED Talk. "First, you should always listen more than you talk on a date. People love to feel heard and understood. Second, don't rush anything. Go at a pace that feels comfortable for both of you. And third, don't be afraid to show your quirks. Be yourself."

"Got it." It's all probably obvious information to some people, but being out of the game for so long, I'm surprised I've even gotten this far with Hannah.

"Oh! And it's rough out there. That's why when you see someone special, you've got to take a leap."

"You think Hannah is special?" Of course, that's my opinion, but I'm eager to hear my closest friend's two cents.

He takes his time thinking about it. "She seems real. Genuine. And that's rare. Plus, the way she looked at you..." He whistles.

My skin heats up. "All right, message received."

"Seriously, it's good you're doing this. It's, uh..."

"What?"

He scratches the back of his neck, looking slightly uncomfortable. "It's been years. I mean, I know you've been with women in that time..."

I look away, not proud of the occasional, casual hookups I've indulged in to take the edge off.

"You haven't dated, though," he finishes. "Right?"

"Right." The word tastes acidic and unwelcome, the whole matter one I've done my best to avoid.

And for the most part, I have successfully avoided it. Being a single parent is a twenty-four-seven job, a great distraction from anything and everything. The day Katie was born, my every cell became devoted to her.

And then, when Talia wasn't there anymore... The rest of existence kind of blurred out. All I saw was the little bubble my kid and I were in. It was us against the world.

"Not every woman is like Talia," Nathan says quietly, as if he can read my mind.

A lump forms in my throat. "I know."

"And it might have been easy to be an antisocial hermit in a big city, but that won't fly here. You have too many people looking out for you."

I snort. "I'd say it's a few too many people. And they're not so much looking out for me as they are trying to crawl up my ass all the time. How am I supposed to have a good date when it feels like the whole damn town is watching us?"

"True." Nathan gazes across the street, his eyes unfocused. "I did say I have some ideas, though."

I push off the truck, standing straighter. "Okay, hit me with it. What is it?"

He looks back at me, his eyes twinkling. "Don't worry. It's a good one."

## *Chapter Nine*

HANNAH

"Whew." The woman who has just selected a pair of crochet needles for her nephew's birthday buttons up her jacket. "What a drop in temperature, hm?"

I force a smile as I ring her up. "Yeah, it's pretty cold."

Actually, it's more like achingly cold. Painfully cold.

I've been feeling the quick change in temperatures since last night, when my joints started protesting. It was hard to get out of bed this morning, and after a long day of work, it's hard to even remember the names of many of the skeins.

The math is pretty simple. A quick weather change equals aching joints, brain fog, and exhaustion. And if I don't take it easy soon, I'll be dealing with a serious flare-up.

Which would mean I'd need to shut the shop down for a day or more. Since Flick has a big order she needs to fulfill this week, I wouldn't have anyone to cover for me for that long.

"Thank you." I hand the woman her bag. "I hope he has a great birthday."

"Thanks, sweetie. Take care." She bustles out of the shop, and I glance at the clock on the wall.

The second I do, I wish I hadn't. It's two more hours until Flick comes in to close for me, and then I have my date with Michael.

Going out with him tonight is pushing it. I know that. Lately, though, he's been the number one thing I think about, and I don't want to miss any opportunities to spend time with him. Plus, I haven't told him I have fibromyalgia, and I still haven't figured out how to bring it up, so that's another reason I don't want to cancel.

It's just all such a mess. I can't close Knit Happens early, because that would alienate some of my customers, and I don't want to miss tonight with Michael either. But if I push my limits and have a flare, everything will fall apart.

Once again, I'm stuck between a rock and a hard place, my condition forcing my life to a standstill.

Tears fill my eyes, and I curl my hands into fists. I quit wondering years ago why I received the random dice-roll that gave me this condition, but I've never stopped being angry. Never stopped imagining where I might be in life if chronic pain weren't constantly in my way.

My cell rings, and I answer Flick's call. "Hey."

"What's wrong?" she asks immediately.

I sigh and sit on the stool behind the counter. Damn, this woman is perceptive—and I was trying to sound chipper. "I'm just tired. The weather is not doing me any favors."

"God, I'm so sorry." There's a pause. "Uh, hold on. I have to, um..."

"Flick?"

The only answer is the sound of vomiting.

"You okay?" I ask.

"Yeah. Fine." Her voice is weak.

I frown. "Oh no. Are you sick?"

"It's just a stomach bug. I'll be okay."

"You can't come in and close."

"No, no. I—"

"Flick," I say, voice hard. "I'll close."

"You're not feeling well either."

It's true, and the thought of being here for four more hours makes me want to sob, but what else can I do? At the end of the day, I'm the only person who's responsible for Knit Happens.

"Your date..."

"I'll reschedule," I say.

"No, you won't. Hang tight, and I'll call you right back." She hangs up before I can answer.

Putting my phone down, I sigh. I should probably be going on a date just as much as I should be working all evening, but if Michael and I do something chill, like dinner or a movie, then I'll be okay. Some warmth and sitting down will serve me well.

The minutes tick by while I do some light straightening up. The thought of wrapping my coat around myself and taking a nap on the floor is tempting, but if I do that, I might not wake up when a customer comes in.

Fifteen long, slow minutes pass, and I'm about to text Flick when the door opens. Maya and Alexis come in with a gust of wind, Alexis carrying a bag of to-go food.

"We're here to close for you," Maya announces.

My jaw drops. "What?"

Alexis puts the bag on the counter and takes off her coat. "We were having dinner down the street when Flick called."

"But... That's..." I can't even formulate a full sentence. I barely know these women, and they've dropped what they're doing to come and save my butt.

"We got this. Go home." Maya pats my shoulder.

"Do we have this?" Alexis's face scrunches. "I don't even know the first thing about running a shop."

"It's pretty straightforward." I blink back tears of gratitude. "You just need to know how to run the register. I'll show you."

Maya's phone rings. "Oh. Hold on. It's Flick." She answers the FaceTime.

"Is she still there?" Flick asks right away.

"Me?" I look over Maya's shoulder.

"Go!" Flick shoos me. "Get ready for your big night."

"I need to show them—"

"I'll stay on the phone and show them everything they need to know. You need to rest for a while before you go out."

Because I don't want to have an argument, I just nod. "Thank you, guys. So much."

"Anytime, girl." Alexis gives me a hug.

After another round of thanks, I grab my things and head outside. It's chilly, though not more than I can bear since I have my warm car and house waiting for me.

Once home in my little cottage, I skip taking a nap and jump right into getting ready. At this point, it makes more sense to keep going and not give my energy a chance to lag.

One quick shower and a makeup application later, I pull on wool leggings under my plaid skirt and pick out some earrings that go with the gold rim of my glasses. My head still feels heavy, and my whole body aches, but with the way my stomach is dancing, I hardly notice.

Stepping back, I inspect myself in the bedroom mirror—right as there's a knock on the front door.

My heart leaping into my throat, I cross the living room, frowning at its condition. Both because I've been busy and not feeling great, the house could do with some tidying up. Unfolded laundry sits in a pile on the couch, and mail is spread across the coffee table.

With that in mind, I don't open the door *all* the way.

"Hi." I block Michael's view of my messy house. I'm sure I'm about to say something else, but my mind just flatlines.

He's not wearing anything special, and it's not like he looks any different. Or does he? Because I don't remember my knees becoming this gelatinous around him.

Is it his smell? Something different about the way he's done his hair? Or am I just falling head over heels for this guy?

"Hey." The soothing balm that is his deep voice washes away all worries about tonight. Just like that, I know everything will go well, simply because I'll be with him. "You look great."

"Oh. Thank you." I smooth my skirt. "Let me just grab my stuff."

Snatching my jacket and purse from their hooks, I step onto the little porch with its swinging bench and hedge that half hides the area from the street. The woman I rent from let the garden grow out of control while she was here, and I haven't had the time or the green thumb to do anything about it.

Not that I mind. The whole spot has a magical, wild feel to it that tickles my heart.

"Where are we going?" I follow him into the gravel driveway, where he's parked behind my car.

"It's a surprise." He opens the truck door for me, and my stomach drops.

*Surprise.*

Most people love that word, but not me. If I don't know where we're going, how will I know whether or not I have the tolerance for it? And if I don't have the tolerance for it and I have a flare-up...

I work to get my breathing under control. "Great."

He doesn't seem to notice my discomfort, instead taking his place behind the wheel and drumming his fingers as he backs out of the driveway. "How was your day?"

My little porch becomes smaller. It's not too late to say that

I can't go, that I'm not feeling well—not too late to make up some excuse about having to do paperwork for the shop or call my aunt.

I can't tell him the truth. Not yet. There's no such thing as a conversation where one person says, "Hey, I might be about to have a fibromyalgia flare," and the second person goes, "Oh, really? You should stay home, then." Most people don't know what fibro is, and others have received all the information and still—somehow—think it's not real. They think the people with it, like me, are being dramatic about the pain, that we're making it up for attention and to get out of hard work.

I squeeze my eyes shut, nausea that has nothing to do with a flare rising in my chest. Michael isn't like that. He's nice. He's considerate. He listens.

He would believe me.

Right?

I pop my eyes open. "It was good. How was yours?"

And there it goes; I've missed my chance to explain myself and escape a potentially bad situation. I've chosen how much I like this guy and fear over what he might say and think if I were to come clean. I'm betting on the chance that tonight will be easygoing and that I'll return home no worse off than I am now.

"Nice," he says. "It was a slow day at the firehouse."

We make small talk about our jobs while he drives across the island. When he reaches the bridge and we enter the mainland, I'm still holding on to some hope. Maybe we're just going to a restaurant over here.

But then he takes a left, and we drive down the coast, deeper and deeper into uncertainty. My stomach knots tighter, and my head starts spinning.

"Surprise." Michael pulls up to a mini golf course.

"Oh. Wow. Cool." I blink and do some quick calculations.

It's about forty degrees out. The wind coming off the ocean blows straight onto the golf course. It's a standing-only activity.

Yep. My odds aren't good at all.

"Come on." He leads me across the parking lot and to the short line to get clubs and balls. "Have you ever played?"

"It's been years." I do my best to sound as excited as he is. Maybe this won't be as bad as I think. We're just walking and standing around after all. It's not like it'll be physically challenging.

By the second hole, though, reality comes crashing in. Everyone else on the course looks perfectly comfy in this weather, but the chill has seeped into my bones, making me shiver. Fire sears through my joints, every cell in my body aches, and I'm so tired that if I sat down on the fake grass, I'd be asleep in seconds.

What's happening isn't foreign. If I don't make it home and into bed within the hour, I'll have a flare. All of my symptoms will get worse, and I'll be stuck in bed for days, unable to sleep from the pain.

I have no choice. I need to tell Michael the truth.

The mere thought is a vise grip around my vocal cords. He looks so proud of himself for bringing me here, and I don't want to rain on his parade. I also wanted to be ready for this conversation, to have a script prepared so that I can make it through without stuttering.

Because, truthfully, I'm terrified. What if he thinks I'm being dramatic? Or that fibromyalgia isn't real?

Then again, is that someone I really want to be with? Isn't it better to rip the Band-Aid off now and expose the truth, whatever it may be?

"Michael." My voice shakes, and his name comes out in a partial croak.

"Uh-huh?" He turns away from where he's about to take

his first shot into the plastic alligator mouth. At the sight of my face, his eyebrows knit. "What's wrong?"

I gulp, the shivers from the cold nothing compared to the trembling in my heart. Here goes nothing. "I need to tell you something. I have fibromyalgia. It's a chronic condition."

"Oh." He blinks and turns more fully to face me. "Okay."

His face is so warm, so receptive, it gives me the courage to go on. "It means pain in your muscles, ligaments, tendons. Fatigue. Headaches. Sensitivity to heat and...cold." The last part is hard to say, because I can't help but worry that it sounds like I'm calling him out for bringing me here—which, of course, I'm not.

His mouth drops open. "I see. Are you not feeling well? It's cold out. Is this too cold for you?"

I bite my bottom lip. "I'm sorry. If I don't go home and go to bed, I'll have a flare right here on the golf course, which means you'll probably need to half carry me to the truck, and then I'll start crying in pain on the way home because just being on the highway will hurt so much, though it'll be nothing like the potholes we'll go over on the island..."

I suck in a deep breath. That was a lot, but I needed to get it all out before I lost my nerve and never gave myself the opportunity to do it again.

"Shit." He takes my club from me. "I'm so sorry I brought you here."

"No, it's okay. You didn't know. I—I didn't tell you." The tears are still threatening to spill over, tears of relief. He's responding even better than I had hoped for.

Not only is he understanding, he's concerned. Gentle.

"Here." He takes off his coat and wraps it around me. "Sit on this bench over here while I bring the truck around."

There's not even time to thank him. He's off at a jog, returning our clubs and balls and then hopping into the truck.

The people playing around us don't seem to notice anything is off, and thank God. There's little that's as embarrassing as this.

"Would you like me to carry you?" He gets down on one knee in front of the bench, a knight in shining armor.

As tempting as it is to be cradled against his strong chest, I also don't want to be stared at. So I shake my head.

"I can walk, thanks."

It's like I've aged sixty years while sitting on the bench. My joints protest against the slightest movement, and I shuffle more than walk my way to the truck. Michael is there the whole time, his arm looped through mine, letting me lean on him.

At the passenger's side door, the step leading up to the seat seems impossibly high. How can I even lift my foot that much?

"Here." Michael hesitates, his arms held out. "May I?"

I nod, too weary to talk. With one smooth motion, he lifts me up and deposits me in the seat. If only I weren't feeling so crummy, I could take the moment to enjoy being in his arms. Instead, the touch causes more pain, and I have to grit my teeth.

But at least the seat is warm, the hot air is blowing in my face. We take off down the highway, Michael driving maybe a little too fast.

"I'll take the newer roads on the island," he says. "Those don't have as many potholes. And you can doze off if you need to."

I nod, my eyelids already heavy, my head rolled to the side. "Thank you."

Only my aunt and Flick have ever been this understanding and attentive to my needs, and that's because they have front-row seats to what this condition is like. But Michael doesn't know that much—at least, I don't think he does—and he's doing what I need anyway. He's not asking questions. He's not demanding proof.

"I can carry you in." His voice breaks through the steady hum of the engine.

Opening my eyes, I see that we're in front of my house. Being carried in would be amazing, but even with all the pain and fatigue, I can't forget the mess that is my house. There could be a zombie apocalypse happening, and I would suggest we stay outside and take our chances rather than have him see my underwear on my bedroom floor and my dishes stacked in the sink.

One day, maybe I won't care about that as much. One step at a time, though. Tonight, I showed him a big part of myself.

"I'll walk you to the door, then." He replies when I don't immediately answer. He comes around to my side of the truck, helps me down, and then stays by my side the whole way to the front porch.

My hands tremble as I get my keys out, so he swipes them from my hands and opens the door. "Can I do anything for you? Bring you anything?"

"No, thank you. I'll be okay." I use the last of my energy to muster a smile—and it's worth it. He smiles back softly, though there's more concern there than anything else.

"Text or call if you need anything. I mean it. Even if it's the middle of the night." He leans forward and kisses me on the forehead. Warmth blossoms where his lips have touched, trickling down my head and neck and into my chest.

"Thank you again." I step inside.

"Anytime, Hannah." His gaze holds mine for a long moment. "It's my pleasure."

Closing the door, I stumble to my bedroom and collapse on the mattress. His kiss still lingers on my skin, a soft promise that he isn't going anywhere, that he's not afraid.

That truth is a warm ember I hold close to my heart as I close my eyes and drift off into nothingness.

*Chapter Ten*

MICHAEL

Sitting at the kitchen table, I click the next link on my tablet, opening up another site. Like everything else online, the topic of fibromyalgia leads to an endless rabbit hole—which I jumped down about an hour ago.

When Hannah brought up the condition, it took me a moment to even properly process the word. I'd never heard it before.

With each sentence I read now, my stomach twists a little tighter. Evidently, it's quite controversial in the medical community. Some doctors don't even believe it exists—which is fucked up, and it's not surprising that it mostly affects women since I know from hearing my mom and sister talk that it's sometimes hard for their health issues to be taken seriously.

One commenter in a thread refers to fibromyalgia being the "new hysteria"—basically a made-up condition that women are using as an excuse to get attention. Shaking my head, I move on.

Fatigue, joint and muscle pain, bad periods, IBS, poor sleep, TMJ... The list of symptoms goes on and on. No one really knows what causes the condition, but from what people say online, it sounds absolutely fucking exhausting.

65

"Like gravity has been turned up and the world is pressing down on you," one person writes. "I'd compare it to going on an unexpectedly long hike with a backpack you can't take off—every day, all day long," another person says.

I sit back in my chair, my jaw tight. Damn. So that's what Hannah experiences *every day?*

Why didn't she tell me sooner?

Then again, why should I expect that? I'm not entitled to know anything about her life, and she was probably worried about how the news would change our dynamic.

Leaning forward, I start a new search: "How to help people fibromyalgia."

The first thing that comes up is the spoon theory. It's all about how people with chronic pain conditions often imagine their energy is measured in spoons, and they have a finite number of these spoons each day. Most daily activities, from small ones like getting dressed to large ones like completing a day at work, require spoons. Once a person runs out of spoons for the day, any additional activities they do might cause a flare. It can take a while for each individual to figure out exactly how many spoons they have per day, and once they do, most people are careful to monitor their usage closely.

Learning this part is a punch to the gut. Hannah and I must have seen mini golf completely differently. For me, it was a relaxing way to spend an evening. In her head, though, she was probably calculating how many spoons the game would require. Maybe she didn't even have any spoons left, but she chose to stay for me.

Sighing, I push my fingers through my hair. So that's two dates I've messed up.

Three strikes and you're out, right? I better make our next night together something special.

I'll tailor this next one to her needs, make sure that every detail is just right, that it will require the least number of spoons possible.

But...how the hell do I do that? How do I figure out what the perfect activity is for someone with fibromyalgia?

The internet can only take me so far. I need insight from people who know Hannah, who are familiar with her interests and energy levels. Which means I'll need to do something I never do, something that I hate.

I'll need to ask around town.

* * *

"Michael, honey. You're early." My mom steps out of the elementary school office to greet me.

I freeze in the hallway. She must have seen me through the glass door. If I'd known she would be in there, I would have taken the other way around.

"Yeah, I want to talk to one of Katie's teachers before school gets out." I stuff my hands into my jeans, hoping she doesn't ask any more questions but knowing she will.

It's not like I was avoiding running into my mother here—she does teach at this school after all—I just would prefer to skip an interrogation. Jenny got it from somewhere, and, well... this is where she got it from.

It doesn't help that the two of them live together, which means it's just a tornado of probing and unsolicited advice over at their house.

"Oh?" Her eyebrows rise. "Who?"

"Maya."

She cocks her head and folds her arms. "Is something going on in art class? Katie—"

"No, it's about something else."

She studies me. "I thought you were seeing the owner of the yarn shop. Are you dating Maya too?"

A couple teachers walk by, glancing at us in interest.

"No, Mom," I say quickly, not wanting to start a rumor about my dating multiple women.

Not that Hannah and I are exclusive. We've only been out a couple times—three, if you count coffee—but I don't want to date anyone else. Most of all, I want Hannah to know that I don't want to.

"Hmm." She's still giving me that look like I've been caught doing something at the back of the classroom I shouldn't be, passing notes or hiding my Game Boy behind my textbook.

It wasn't fun when I was her actual student twenty-five years ago, and it isn't fun now.

"I'll see you later." I walk past her.

"Oh. Michael," she calls out, but I'm already around the corner and pretending like I don't hear.

A part of me feels guilty about that, but I didn't come here to catch up with family. I came here for information.

Maya's classroom door is propped open and empty, but I knock on it anyway. She looks up from where she's standing at her desk, a brown-haired young woman that I've spotted working the drop-off and pickup lines.

"Hello," she says softly.

"Hi." I take a cautious step into the classroom, not wanting to intrude too much on her space without an invitation. "I'm—"

"Michael. Katie's dad."

"Yeah." My shoulders relax. If she knows I'm Katie's dad, does that mean she knows I'm dating Hannah? According to Jenny, Maya has been going to Hannah's crafting group for women with chronic pain.

What sort of condition does Maya have? Looking at her

now, she doesn't seem any different from anyone else. But that's just a reminder that we never truly know what people are going through. We can take a quick glance at someone and make all kinds of assumptions that don't even come close to hitting the mark.

"Is this an all right time?" I ask. There aren't any students in her room, so I'm praying that I've scored when it comes to timing.

"It's perfect. This is my planning period for the week."

I clear my throat. "I wanted to ask you some questions… about Hannah."

Her eyes widen. "Oh. Sure. Is everything okay?"

"Yeah, yeah. I just…" I shift my weight, surprised at how nervous I am. "We've gone out on a few dates, and I would really like to get your advice on…on planning a date that works for someone with chronic pain."

I duck my head, suddenly realizing just how I've put her on the spot. By asking about Hannah, I've inadvertently brought up Maya's own chronic condition—whatever that may be. And perhaps she doesn't want anyone to even know about it.

When I look up, though, she's smiling. "That's amazing."

"Really?" My voice pitches.

"Yes. Have a seat." She pulls a chair over to her desk. "I don't know how much Hannah has told you…"

"Just that she has fibromyalgia. I've read some online, but I wanted to get advice from, uh, someone who really knows."

Again, thank God, she doesn't seem put off. "Okay, so warmth is key. So is food. It's hard to have the energy to do anything if your physical needs aren't met."

From my pocket, I take out the pen and small notebook I brought along and jot down notes. "Great. What else?"

"No physically taxing activities."

"What would be considered taxing?" I ask, already afraid I'll screw that up. As of last night, I wouldn't have considered mini golf taxing for anyone who can walk.

Maya lays it all out on the table, giving me more tips than I was even prepared for. By the time I need to leave her room to pick up Katie from the front of the school, and after I've thanked Maya maybe a dozen times, I finally feel equipped to meet Hannah's needs.

"Dad!" Spotting me come out of the school, Katie runs up. "Can we go to the bookstore? There's a new comic I want."

I consider our to-do list, filled with dinner, chores, and her bedtime routine. "Sure. We can drop by for a few minutes. Let's go." Maybe they will have a book on fibromyalgia.

"Yes!" She bounces up and down as we walk to the truck.

"How was your day?"

"Good," she says, clambering into her seat and buckling up. "How was yours?"

"Great, and getting even better." I catch my reflection in the rearview mirror. My grin wide, I look like someone I don't recognize. A new man.

And maybe I'm exactly that.

## *Chapter Eleven*

HANNAH

The streetlights pop on up and down my block, and the German shepherd across the street barks in excitement at his owner coming home from work. It's another calm evening in another small town on a small island.

Standing up from my swinging bench, I walk across the porch, my stomach twisting. When I moved to Pine Island, the only dream I had involved my shop. I didn't let myself think too much about fitting into a community or finding love. And now...

Taking a deep breath, I lean against the railing, my heart racing from both anxiety and excitement. Two days of not seeing Michael feel like a lot, but even though I managed to avoid a flare the other night, I'm still on edge.

He's shown how caring he is, how attentive. And yet, I'm still afraid.

Maybe it's because I'm not used to things going this well and a part of me is always on edge, waiting for this new relationship to crash and burn.

Headlights slice across my yard, and Michael's truck pulls into the driveway. My stomach just about climbs up my throat, and I tug on my sweater and smooth my hair, not sure what to do with myself.

He steps out of his truck, a hunky specimen of a man, his long legs eating up the distance between the driveway and me.

It's not until he's on my bottom step that he finally speaks. "Hi."

"Hello," I squeak. "How are you?"

"Great, now that I'm here." The way he says it, it doesn't sound like a line. It sounds like the words he's been holding in all day, just waiting for the moment when he can finally release them to the universe.

Taking my hand, he leads me to his truck. I suppose I walk, but I don't remember even taking one step. Everything is hazy with my fingers around his, and the next thing I know, we're driving out of town.

Again.

"Tonight is fibro-friendly," Michael announces.

"Oh. Okay. Thank you." What could we possibly be doing outside of town that won't drain my energy?

I bite my bottom lip, an unexpected swell of emotion crashing through me. Maybe it's delusional to think I can even date. Someone like Michael—fit, active—would probably be happier with a woman who can keep up with him. I can't handle more than a walk around the block or a yin yoga session, and there are more soft bits on me than muscle.

"I did my research." Pride buoys his words. "This will be a calm, no-stress night."

That makes me relax—until we park in front of what looks like a small fishing shack. Trees crowd around it on two sides, with the beach on another. There's electricity, at least, and the porch light is on.

But what the heck are we doing here? Are we going out on the water? Exploring the beach at night?

My heart hits my rib cage with the force of a sledgehammer, over and over. It's too cold on the beach and the water.

Michael turns to me, grinning—until he sees my face. "Shit. What is it?"

I lick my lips and consider just burying my fears and not making a big deal out of anything, but I've learned enough to know that will get me nowhere but into a flare. "I'm worried about a repeat of last time."

"Ah. I see." He turns to face me more directly, and his scent envelops me in a spicy embrace. "Tell you what. I'll open the shack's door, and if you don't like what you see, we'll turn right back around and I'll drop you off at home."

I nod slowly. He did say that tonight was fibro-friendly, and it would be unfair of me not to give him the benefit of the doubt. Not living with this condition doesn't mean he can't understand it.

We leave the truck, and he leads me to the little shack. After Michael unlocks it, the door creaks open, and the sight inside literally takes my breath away.

A big, cozy couch with blankets and throw pillows is pushed against the wall, a small projector on a shelf above it. Serving-size snacks fill a bowl on a coffee table, and twinkle lights give the whole place a soft glow. The space heater is going full blast, and the curtains are closed to keep the rest of the world out.

"Wow," I breathe, stepping into the room.

"You like it?" His voice comes from so close behind me, I feel a delicious tickle on the back of my neck.

"It's wonderful." I nod at the white sheet hanging across from the couch. "Are we watching something?"

"That was my thought. Or we can just hang out. There are snacks, and here's a cooler with different drinks." He walks around the room, pointing everything out. "If you'd like something hot, there's an electric kettle. I can make you tea or hot chocolate."

I bite into my smile. "Michael…"

"And here's a footrest." He pulls it out. "Or you can lie on the couch. I can sit on the floor. Are these enough blankets?" He picks up a stack of at least five.

My grin turns into a laugh. "It's more than enough. Thank you. So much."

The gratitude filling my heart is enough to make me cry. Tonight clearly took some time and effort to put together, and being a single dad and a fire chief, he's probably chronically short on that.

"I wanted to make sure you're comfortable." He hangs his coat on a rack and gestures for mine. "And to have an evening where we don't feel like the whole town is watching."

"That's certainly a bonus." I hand him my coat and settle on one end of the couch.

"I preselected a few shows I thought you might like, but we don't need to stick with them." His leg brushes mine as he passes by on the way to the other end of the couch, and electricity crackles under my skin. "There's a Scandinavian knitting competition that's dubbed in English, the latest season of *The Great British Sewing Bee*, or *Gravity Falls*."

"*Gravity Falls*?" I cock my head at him. "Isn't that a kids show?"

He looks sheepish. "Well, yeah, but one of the characters is constantly knitting. And it's more like a show for everyone. Katie and I both like it."

"Sounds good." Once more, I take in the room—this little oasis that Michael wove together just for us. I want to say thank you again, but I don't want to cheapen the expression, so I settle with putting it another way. "This is really special."

He visibly relaxes another degree. "I was so nervous about

getting this right. Although...I'm only now realizing that I should have picked at least one show that wasn't knitting-themed. I know that's not your whole identity." He cringes.

"Actually, sometimes it feels like it is. It got me through a really hard time—my symptoms starting and not knowing what I had, my breakup..." The diagnosis, which came after a few years, was welcome, but not the saving grace I'd hoped for.

Since there's no cure for fibromyalgia, you basically just learn to live with it, to manage it. You adjust. You change your expectations for life.

"I spent a lot of time on my aunt's couch during a bad period." Thinking about those weeks is bittersweet. They were hard at the time, but they turned out to be the launching pad to where I am now. "She taught me how to knit while I was there, and the rest is kind of history. It was hard to keep up with teaching anyway with my symptoms, and when I saw the store-front online..."

"It was meant to be," he finishes softly.

Something glimmers in his eye, an understanding or a knowing that I can't quite get a read on.

"Yeah," I whisper.

He nods. "I felt that way when Katie was born, like I'd waited my whole life to be a dad. When she came into the world, it was like, this is it. This is what I'm here for."

"That's beautiful." I can't help it; I need to know. "Can I ask about her mother? Where is she?"

His face hardens. "She left. Not long after Katie was born. It was...challenging for her to be a mother. She got pregnant pretty early in our relationship and we tried to make it work that whole year, but it just wasn't who she is."

"Oh." My eyelashes flutter. This is so heavy. How do I even follow that up?

"They don't have contact. The last that I heard from Talia

was when Katie was one. I sent her some photos, and she wrote back, asking me not to get in touch again. Said it was too hard."

My chest aches with pain for both Michael and Katie. The poor girl. What must it be like, growing up knowing you weren't wanted by your mother?

"I don't hate Talia for it," Michael says, and it's more like he's speaking to himself than me at this point. "Well...most of the time, I don't. Parenthood was thrust on us both. I took to it, she didn't. Would I rather Katie has a mother? Of course, but no mother is better than one who doesn't want to be there." He blinks, as if coming out of a trance. "I'm sorry. That was a lot. I shouldn't—"

"No, it's okay." I touch his knee. "My mom died when I was eight. I went to live with my aunt."

His eyes widen. "Wow, Hannah, I'm so sorry."

A lump forms in my throat. "Thank you. My aunt is like my mom, though, so I'm really fortunate to have her."

We sit in silence, the weight of the past pressing in around us. It feels more bearable now, though. It's not like we're carrying each other's loads, but we're acknowledging what the other person has been through—we're really seeing each other —and that makes everything feel easier.

Michael's gaze holds mine, and the air between us becomes charged. We're about a foot away, so close I would only need to lean forward...

Except I lose my nerve and look away.

If he's disappointed, I can't see it. He stands and messes with the projector. "Check out the snacks. There should be some there you like."

I cock my head at that. "How do you know what snacks I like?"

"Being in a small town has some benefits," he chuckles.

Indeed, it does, because inside the bowl—along with pretzels, hummus, popcorn, and veggie sticks—is a paper bag with the coffee shop's rhubarb crumble cookies—my favorite. He must have asked the staff there what I usually get.

"How can you be this thoughtful?" I blurt out before I even know what I'm saying.

He stops whatever he's doing with the projector and looks down at me. "Isn't that what I'm supposed to be? What have the other men you've dated been like?"

I snort. "You don't want to hear me talk about that."

"I want to hear everything about your life—as long as you're comfortable sharing it."

God, how did I get so lucky? Why, out of all people in the world, am *I* here tonight with this amazing man?

"My last boyfriend didn't believe fibromyalgia is real," I say, Michael's warmth giving me courage. "He didn't even believe the doctor who explained it to him. He called the man a quack."

Michael's eyes widen, and he plops down on the couch. "Seriously? What an asshole." He makes a face. "Sorry."

"No, it's okay. He was an asshole. He told me that I just wasn't pushing hard enough and that everyone is tired and I should toughen up." My lips draw tight.

"Please tell me you punched him for that."

"No," I laugh. "But I did break up with him in the parking lot after that doctor's appointment."

"Good." He nods seriously. "You deserve so much more than that, Hannah. You deserve..." His face turns pink.

"What?" I can't get my voice above a whisper. "What do I deserve?"

His throat rolls with a swallow. "To be seen."

The words break down a wall I didn't know I had, and suddenly, the power of a thousand horses is behind me. Leaning forward, I press my lips to his.

He responds immediately, his kiss gentle but firm. Slow, like we have all the time in the world. It's also over too soon.

He pulls back, gazing at me with heavy eyes. I'm aching for his touch, but also glad that he's giving me space, taking things slow. After all my dormant years, I can't just jump into something hot and heavy.

"So," he says. "How did I do?"

"With the kiss?"

He chuckles. "With setting up tonight. And...sure, with the kiss."

I pretend to think about it, though I already know the answer. "Ten out of ten."

He whistles. "You're blowing smoke."

"Maybe I am, maybe I'm not." I pointedly look at the projector, though I'm smiling.

He turns on *Gravity Falls*, and through a whole four episodes, my smile never wavers. My rating might have sounded like an exaggeration, but it wasn't. It was pure truth.

Because that's all that's here between me and Michael. Sweet, innocent truth. A place where I can show up and be my full, authentic self.

God, does it feel good.

## *Chapter Twelve*

HANNAH

Hunched over in front of Knit Happens's counter, I type away. It's been another busy week, but at least I'm finally working on my funding application.

Between running the shop, organizing a class I've been offered to teach at the mainland elementary school, and pacing myself, it's been hard to create time to fill out the documents and write my essay, and it's nice to finally be making some progress.

And not just when it comes to my business.

The few days since Michael took me to the cozy fishing shack, I've been floating around on cloud nine. We haven't been able to spend any significant time together since, but he's popped into the shop to say hello a couple times and we've been texting constantly.

That night at the fishing shack felt like the start of a new chapter in my life. One where I can not only be myself, but where I'm supported in it. And that kiss...

It still makes me weak in the knees to think about it.

Yet, even though everything is going well, the fear is still there. It's not unfounded either. At any moment, a flare could come along and ruin all my progress in life. Though I can get ahead of most of them by pacing myself, they do occasionally pop up out of the blue without any warning.

It's a flare like those that could cause me to shut down the shop for days and lose money and customers. A flare that could alienate Michael when he sees just how bad things can get with me.

Yes, he cares. Yes, he is doing his best to be supportive and understanding. But that doesn't change the fact that you need to see someone at their worst before you get an idea of who they really are. And my worst is not pretty.

It's a burden. The kind that I would never ask anyone to carry with me.

My phone comes to life with a call from my aunt, and I snatch it up. "Hey, Carol."

"Hey, sweetie. I have a surprise."

"You do? What?"

"I'm coming to visit you!"

I try not to drop the phone. "You...uh... What do you mean? When?"

"I have a flight booked for tomorrow morning. Now, I know what you're going to say, and I promise I won't be a burden on you—"

"No, I don't think that. It's just—"

"I'm coming to help, Hannah. Your plate is full. That last flare sounded like it was really bad, and I know you were downplaying it for my benefit."

That shuts me up, and I pull my lips tight. Yes, I did downplay it. But only because I don't want her to worry herself sick about me when she's on the other side of the country and there's nothing she can do.

"I'm coming to help," she repeats. "Not to be a guest or to

expect you to entertain me. I can help at the shop. What do you think of that?"

Her help would be amazing. Of course I need it.

But Carol can be...a lot when it comes to her concern for me. Maybe because she's retired now and doesn't have a lot to do, or maybe losing her sister so young has made her afraid the same thing will happen with me.

I don't know, but I do know that I could use her help, and I'm too proud to ask for it. "That would be nice. Thank you. I don't want you to wear yourself out here, though."

"I could never do that. You know me. I have more energy than I know what to do with."

I chuckle. Don't I know it.

"I'll send you my flight info," she says. "Don't worry about picking me up from the airport. I'll get myself to Pine Island."

"You sure?"

"One hundred percent. I'll see you soon."

"See you soon. Love you."

She sends a kissing sound and hangs up. Already, a bit of weight lifts off my shoulders. My aunt's help around the shop will be invaluable, but I'll need to be careful not to take advantage of it. While she tends to give endlessly, it doesn't feel right always accepting her help. I would hate to be the reason that she gets burned out.

The door opens, and I look up from my laptop. Flick walks in carrying a basketful of new yarns. "Hey," she says.

"Hi." I close my computer. Is it really time for the crafting group to start? Where did the afternoon go?

"What's wrong?"

"Nothing." I force myself to smile.

"Right." She puts her basket down and shrugs out of her coat. "I know you well enough. Don't tell me you weren't just sitting here worrying yourself half to death over something."

Sighing, I get up and start putting down the big cushions Flick and I picked up the other day, which are way more comfortable than the folding chairs I was using.

"Things are good. My aunt is coming to visit. She's going to help around the shop."

"Oh, really? That's awesome! How long is she staying for?"

I laugh. "Probably until I force her to leave."

My laughter dies down, and I remember just how fortunate I am. Not everyone has someone like Carol in their lives, and considering the fact that I started out as the kid of a single mom then became an orphan, I'm pretty damn lucky to have ended up with such an amazing woman raising me.

"So, things are good," Flick slowly says, and I know there's more coming. "But you're still off. I can see it. What's really up?"

I sigh. "It sucks feeling like I'm always waiting for the next flare, you know? Everything is going well in life, but I'm still on edge."

She nods. "I know what you mean." She gets comfortable on a bright-pink cushion with gold tassels. "Do you want to talk to the group about it tonight? If anyone can understand, it'll be people brought together through chronic pain."

"Yeah," I mumble, though I don't feel certain.

Even though the whole group has so much in common, it's still easier for me to stay quiet. To keep out of the way and not disturb anyone with my fibro problems. It's almost become a survival mechanism at this point—stay quiet and don't rock the boat.

I don't have long to dwell on it, though, because Maya and Alexis arrive, and then a few minutes later, a woman in her early thirties, who introduces herself as Devin and shares that she is a yoga teacher and physiotherapist who has chronic fatigue syndrome.

Having a new person join our ranks buoys my spirit, making me feel like I've done something really special by starting this group, so when Flick raises her eyebrows at me, silently reminding me to share what we were talking about earlier, I don't feel as much resistance.

"Does anyone ever worry—or...more like obsess...over when their next flare will happen?" I casually ask.

The other four look up from the totes they're crocheting, and everyone starts talking at once.

"All the time," Alexis says.

"I didn't even know if I could come tonight." Devin sighs and puts down her crochet hooks. "I couldn't make the first meeting because I couldn't get off the couch."

Maya shakes her head. "It's awful making plans and not knowing if you'll actually be able to honor them or not."

"Right?" Flick says. "Then there's the whole work and career thing. How are we supposed to move ahead in the world when we don't know when we'll next be knocked on our butts?"

"It's hard even when you're a freelancer." Alexis reclines on a stack of cushions, her deft fingers making quick progress on her tote. "I still don't know how much work to schedule for myself week to week. If I were to schedule in anticipation of a flare every week, I wouldn't be able to make enough to pay my bills. So, I end up just having to apologize to clients and turn things in late. I hate it."

"Every time I schedule a yoga workshop," Devin says, eyes wide, "I nearly have a panic attack. What if I have a flare that day, and I have to cancel on everyone? Some people have driven hours to some of my workshops."

Even though everything they're saying is depressing as hell, it's also comforting. This life might be uncertain, but at least I have people around who get it.

"Thank you, you guys," I murmur. "I needed to hear this."

"You're not alone." Flick nudges me with her shoulder.

"Ooh, speaking of not alone…" Alexis's eyes sparkle. "I heard that you and Michael had some alone time at the McGraw fishing shack."

I can only laugh and bury my face in my hands. Is nothing private on this island?

"So, how did it go?" Alexis asks.

"It was amazing." My face warms as I share how Michael dressed up the shack to make it comfortable for me. When I get to the part about the kiss, the shop nearly explodes from the force of the girls' whoops and cheers.

"How was it?" Maya asks.

"Probably perfect," Alexis answers.

"He's the fire chief, right?" Devin's eyes widen. "Oh wow. He's cute. Nice going, Hannah."

"Okay, okay." I bite my smile, my face still hot as I desperately look for a new subject. "Flick brought in some new yarns to test out."

"Hey, the firehouse's annual fundraiser is coming up," Maya says. "Would anyone like to make things we can donate for the raffle? I know I'm not great yet, but my scarf is coming along pretty well."

Everyone chimes in with agreement, and even though it's not a complete topic change—since Michael is still a part of the conversation—I go with it.

"I have some hats I can donate." Putting my needles down, I go to the box behind the counter that I keep personal projects in.

"Wonderful." Maya beams. "And you can go to the fire station to register our contribution, right?"

I freeze, all eyes on me. The girls are setting me up, of course

—and they love it. Even Devin, who is new to the group, is biting back a smile.

"Sure." I gulp. "I'll go."

Flick checks her phone. "You should go now, before it gets dark."

Alexis giggles. "Yes, go now, so we can have a full report when you come back."

"N-now?" My stammer, so obvious, couldn't be more embarrassing.

"He's there," Devin supplies. "I saw him in the window when I walked by."

I lick my dry lips. Michael won't be the only person there. The place will be filled with firefighters I don't know. What if... But maybe... I really should—

"I, uh..."

The girls push me to the door. "Say hi for us," Flick says.

My own shop door slams closed behind me, and I'm left alone on the front stoop.

"Damn it," I mutter.

## Chapter Thirteen

MICHAEL

After making my marks along the wall where the new counter will go, I jot down the measurements and step back to get a visual.

It's usually something I'm good at—imagining a space completely redone before one part is even changed. With the firehouse's kitchen, though, I'm hitting a wall. I can't see anything other than what's in front of me.

Rubbing the back of my neck, I sigh. My frustration has been mounting ever since I walked into this room twenty minutes ago, and though it may be best to throw in the towel for the night, I can't find it in myself to do that. The more challenging a task is, the more I want to overcome it.

There's a knock on the open door, and Nathan strides in with a six-pack. "You look like you're doing some hard math."

I smirk. "That's one way to put it."

"I'll help you out. Two plus two is four." Grinning with self-pleasure, he tosses me a beer.

"Nice." I roll my eyes. "Who let this clown in here?"

"Eh, your team is all sitting in the bay watching the traffic go by. I slipped in completely unnoticed."

Popping the beer can, I take a long sip. "Thanks for this."

"I didn't know if you'd still be here." He settles into one of the plastic chairs around the table. "Isn't your shift over?"

"Yeah, but I need to work on this." I jerk my head at nowhere in particular.

"What about Hannah?"

The name releases a swarm of butterflies that flutter through my chest. "What about her?"

"I thought you might be with her. Or did it not go well at the fishing shack?"

I wouldn't be able to stop my grin if I tried. "It went really well."

"Oh?" He leans back and crosses his legs at the ankles. "Do tell."

I rub the back of my neck, trying to collect my thoughts. But how can words express just how good it feels to be around her—how light, how carefree? Even when we're talking about serious topics, it feels like a huge weight has been lifted from my shoulders and I'm free to just be myself for once.

"I'm falling for her," I say, the words surprising even me. I'm not usually so forthcoming with my feelings.

Nathan slaps his knee. "Hell yeah. Now that's what I want to hear."

My phone rings, and I scramble to pull it from my pocket. *Hannah?*

But it's Pat, who owns Pine Island's hardware store.

"I've got to take this," I mumble, hitting the answer button. "Hey, Pat. Is there something wrong with my order?"

"Hi there, Michael. Well, not exactly..." He trails off, and I frown. "I'm not sure about some of the fittings you want for the kitchen. The faucet you picked out won't work, son."

Closing my eyes, I hold back a groan. Is he being serious?

"I'm sure it will work just fine. A faucet is a faucet. They all carry water."

"Why aren't you just going with the plans your dad made?"

There it is. The ole "Why aren't you just like your dad?" Of course, people find a multitude of ways to say it, to let me know they wish my dad were still here and I was not—poorly, in everyone's specific opinions—stepping into his shoes.

"Because I'm the one working on the kitchen now." I grit my teeth, doing what I can to keep my temper in check. Pat was my dad's closest friend, but trying to micromanage this kitchen renovation is not a healthy way to deal with grief.

I decide against suggesting he give therapy a whirl and wait until I'm sure my voice is even and calm. "Thank you for the input. I'll give it some thought. For now, though, let's go with the faucet I picked out."

He grumbles some under his breath but at least says good-bye. Hanging up, I turn to Nathan.

"You know what would be nice?"

"What?" He slurps his beer.

"If everyone would stop second-guessing every decision I make that even slightly deviates from what my dad might have done. The man wasn't perfect, but now that he's gone, people are worshiping him."

Nathan is quiet for a long moment. "Does any of your frustration have to do with what your dad said the last time you spoke?"

I physically recoil. "What?"

Nathan shrugs. "If you didn't have a button to push, everyone putting their noses in your business wouldn't be so hurtful. It would be easier to shrug it all off. Do you think a part of you believes you really aren't doing a good enough job? Just like how your dad suggested you weren't raising Katie right?"

I cross my arms. "He didn't suggest it. He flat-out stated it."

Damn Nathan. He's too smart sometimes, and as much as I don't want to admit it at this moment, he's right.

"I think about that fight every day." It was the last time we ever spoke, and of course I have regrets.

For months—even following my dad's heart attack in the middle of a fiery house—I've resented him for basically telling me I was failing my daughter. I mean, seriously? Me?

I was the parent who stayed when her mother peaced out. I was the person who sat up with a colicky baby, who arranged my work schedule so I could pick her up from school every day, who passed over every opportunity at finding another relationship or pursuing anything in life that would make me less than fully available to her.

I gave up who I was for Katie, and I would do it again and again in a heartbeat. I live for that kid, and I wouldn't have it any other way.

So, for someone—my own father, at that—to say that I fucked up...

I shake my head. "I moved her back here."

"Because your dad wanted you to?"

My sigh is so heavy it hurts my ribs. "Because he was right. We were too isolated in Seattle." I can at least separate the truth from personal offenses—sometimes.

"And she's happy here. That's what it looks like, anyway."

"Yeah." I chew that over. "But I sometimes think we swung too far in the other direction. It's hard to get a moment alone here."

The front doorbell rings, and I smirk. There's my confirmation from the universe.

"Like so."

"How do you know it's not a real emergency?" Nathan chuckles.

"That's what 9-1-1 is for."

Leaving my beer on the table, I head out of the kitchen and to the front door to see who needs what now. When I open the door, though, my jaw loosens and my stomach bursts into fireworks. It's an instant mood change.

Because Hannah is standing on the firehouse's front steps.

Except it's hard to tell if she's coming or going. She's half turned toward the street, her hands jammed into her jacket pockets.

"O-oh," she stammers. "Hey—hi."

"Hey." The grin that pulls at my lips is as natural and expected as the rising sun. "You're not leaving, are you?"

Her throat rolls with a swallow. "I thought that it might not be a good time."

She glances at the open bay, where music blares from the speakers. We can't see the crew in there, but no doubt they noticed her arrive and have a spy posted up somewhere, gathering information.

"It's a great time," I rush to say, afraid that if I'm not quick enough, she'll turn tail and bound away like a spooked deer.

Her flightiness and anxiety don't bother me, though. They make me more eager to be around her, to take care of her in whatever way she most needs at the moment.

"Come on in." I hold the door open, and she cautiously enters.

"I'm here to register for the fundraiser. For the raffle." She turns to me, and her floral scent tickles my nose, making my body react in a way that it never should while at work. "My friends and I would like to donate some scarves and hats that we've knit."

"That's amazing. Thank you."

She shrugs. "It's not much."

"It's perfect. I'll get you the form to fill out."

I don't get a chance to move, because Nathan comes into the hallway. "Hey, Hannah. How's it going?"

"Good. Thank you." She shifts her weight, looking nervous. "How are you?"

"Busy. Just got a call about a roadside breakdown. They need a tow." He claps me on the shoulder. "See you later."

I'm not sold that he really did receive a call, but it doesn't matter. He's a good friend, giving Hannah and me some privacy yet again—especially since I was just griping about how I don't get enough of it.

"Let's go to the kitchen. We've been moving some things around, and the forms are in there while we organize the office."

On the way, I grab the remote and turn down the speakers in the bay. In the kitchen, I click off the TV show Nathan put on. Hannah finally relaxes a little bit as some silence surrounds us, and I give myself a mental pat on the back. She clearly thrives in low-stimulation environments, and who could blame her? This firehouse is like a circus on the calmest days.

"Have a seat." I pull a raffle registration form out of the filing cabinet and hand it to her along with a pen. "Can I get you a drink?"

"No, thanks." She bends her head and quickly fills out the form—too quickly. I can't have her leave yet, not when she only just got here. I know she has her knitting group to get back to, but, selfishly, I want to hang on to her as long as possible.

She looks around the kitchen. "I thought there would be more people here."

"They're in the bay or catching up on sleep in the bunks upstairs. It's just you and me in this part."

"Oh." Her shoulders drop a little lower. "I thought the place would be full of people, and it freaked me out."

"Why?" I blurt out, then hope that didn't come across as insensitive.

"I'm not great with crowds of strangers." She chuckles. "Or crowds, period. A few people in the store at one time I can handle, but any more than that is...a lot. It's why I always skip the monthly town meetings."

"I get that." I blow out a breath.

Her eyes light up. "You don't like crowds either?"

"Well...it's fine when I don't know the people."

"Ah. I see." She nods and hands me the paper.

"So, uh—" I clear my throat. "How was your day?"

"Good. My aunt is coming tomorrow for a visit. She's going to help around the shop."

"That's great." Unexpectedly, my heart races a little. Will I get to meet this aunt? I don't know why, but it matters to me. I guess I really want to see this woman who's been such an integral part of Hannah's life.

And, what's more, I want her to like me.

"Have you had dinner yet?" I ask, proud of myself for coming up with an excuse for her to stay. "We have a ton of leftover chili. I was about to heat some up."

"Sure. That would be nice." She grabs her phone from her jacket pocket. "I just need to tell Flick to lock up without me."

While she texts, I pull out the chili, get it going on the stove, and serve Hannah one of the beers Nathan brought. Her presence is one simple adjustment, but it makes all the difference in the world. The room that only a few minutes ago was causing so much stress now feels like a sanctuary, a place where I can hide away with the woman I'm crazy about.

With my back turned to Hannah, I grin as I pour the chili into two bowls. Damn, that's right. I'm totally crazy for her.

When was the last time I felt this way about a woman?

Was it...ever?

I certainly haven't gotten romantically involved with anyone since Katie's mom, and our relationship was more hot and cold than anything else. Before that, I was just a boy, jumping from girl to girl, never thinking beyond what the weekend held.

But now, I'm thinking into the future. Dreaming about what next month, next year, looks like with Hannah in my life. It's not just taking care of Katie and running this firehouse—though I'm proud to do those things. It's more.

Life with Hannah is something that's just for *me*. A selfish bubble that I get to escape to every time we're together.

"What are you smiling about?" she asks as I take the seat next to her.

"What's not to smile about right now?"

She ducks her face, but it does nothing to hide her pleased grin. "Oh. I see."

The conversation turns to catching up as we eat, though there's little to catch up on. We've been texting almost nonstop, and it's only our busy schedules that have stopped me from nailing down another date.

But here we are, paths crossed again. You'd almost think it was fate.

"I'll get the dishes," she says once we're finished.

"No, I..."

Her hand has brushed mine, and suddenly, I've forgotten all English. We're standing next to the table, only inches between us. It's like the color intensity has been turned up on the world. I can see her every eyelash, track her every breath.

Putting down my bowl, I take a small step toward her.

Her gaze locks on mine, and the next thing I know, she's between me and the wall, my arms on either side of her head. I'm moving like it's the most natural thing in the world, water following to the sea, my lips dropping to hers.

Her soft mouth welcomes me, opening like petals on the sweetest rose. Heat unfurls from our tongues, and I deepen the kiss, sliding my hands through her hair and down her shoulders.

She grips my t-shirt, twisting it in her palms. A primal hunger awakens in my belly, and I shuffle closer till she's pinned against the wall.

Then someone loudly clears their throat.

Quick as a whip, I step back from Hannah, taking my grabby hands with me. Red and Meg, two of my firefighters, stand in the kitchen doorway.

"If you two are done," Red says, "we'd love to get our dinner."

Hannah blushes and presses her fingers to her lips.

"Go ahead." I gesture to the fridge, then grab Hannah's hand and lead her into the hallway. "I'm sorry," I say the second we're out of earshot.

Fuck, I'm such an idiot. She expressed how worried she was about people being around, and then I went and practically pawed her in a common area.

"It's okay." Her voice is breathy, and she presses so close that her hip bumps against my leg. "How much longer are you here for?"

My pulse quickens. "I can leave whenever. My shift is over."

She bites her lip, already slightly swollen from kissing. "Would you like to come over to my house?"

The question sets off an earthquake that trembles through my bones. Is she asking what I think she is?

I haven't been with a woman in a few years, though, of course, I've thought about what it would be like with Hannah —a lot.

"If you can," she adds. "I know you have Katie—"

"She's at a sleepover tonight, so yes." I find her hand. "I would love to come over."

Her lashes flutter. "Perfect. We can walk there."

"Perfect," I echo.

But will it be? She's just asked me to take our relationship to another level. What if I can't adequately show up? What if tonight just proves that I'm not the man she wants or needs?

Then that's it. End game for us.

"You okay?" she asks.

"Yeah." Pulling myself together, I nod. "Perfect."

That's right. Maybe if I keep saying that word, the night will end up being exactly that.

Somehow.

*Chapter Fourteen*

HANNAH

My heart slams against my rib cage, so fast I wouldn't be able to count the beats if I tried.

Michael is coming over to my house.

*My* house. With me.

And though I didn't say it explicitly, I think he knows that I don't want him over to watch a movie.

Cutting through the empty lot behind the grocery store, we dip down Cedar Lane, a dirt pathway that's been on the island since the town was established and that runs between two rows of buildings. It's a charming shortcut to my house, and I usually take it to work unless I'm running late and need to drive.

We don't speak as we walk, but the air vibrates—and not just between us. The whole island feels charged, the clouds above us churning as dark slips across downtown. Michael's hand finds mine, and peace washes through me.

This is right. So right.

I haven't been with a man since Paul. There hasn't even been anyone I've wanted to be with. Until now.

"Hey, Hannah!"

I jump at the cheery voice, and Michael and I grind to a halt in the middle of the path. Estelle, my elderly neighbor, emerges from behind her giant metal chicken—one of many flamboyant pieces of art in her yard.

"Looks like rain." She wipes her face with the back of her gardening glove.

"Sure does."

She smiles at Michael. "How are you, Michael?"

"Great. I hope you are."

I wait for his hand to tighten on mine, for the indication that he's uncomfortable, thinking about how tomorrow the whole town will be saying that Estelle saw him going into my house. But it never comes. His gentle hold remains steady.

He's proud to be seen with me.

A smile pulls at my lips. Even though I'm still nervous, I suddenly can't wait another minute to get inside my house.

"Well, see you later." I wave at Estelle and practically pull Michael into my yard and through my back door.

I'm shaking with need, my legs weak and my head spinning. A terrible ache fills my core, and there's only one person who can satisfy it.

Shutting the door, I spin to face him. "This is my house."

"It's cute." His eyes never leave my face.

"There's no dirty laundry on the floor today, so that's a win. I figured I wouldn't die of embarrassment if you came over." I'm babbling from nerves, and the more I talk, the faster the words just spit out. "Would you like some tea? Or anything else? It's a little dark in here, isn't it?"

"I think it's perfect," he growls.

He advances on me, head ducked, and the instant his lips meet mine, all anxiety washes away. I'm back in that sacred realm his touch always brings me to, back in a place where nothing could ever be wrong.

The kiss intensifies, and we walk into the living room, lips still locked, arms around each other. I kick my shoes off, and he follows suit. The need that before was a burning ember in my lower belly is now a roaring fire in my every cell.

"I need you," I gasp against his mouth, truer words having never been said.

He growls in response and, in one swift move, picks me up and carries me down the short hallway and into my bedroom.

"Is this the right room?" he asks, not even looking.

I laugh against his jaw. "Bingo."

He sets me gently on the bed and lowers his firm, large body over mine, being careful not to put too much weight on me. Too careful, maybe.

I want him inside me *now,* want it fast and furious till I can't think straight. Even if that's not what's best for my sensitive body.

He takes his time, though, kissing down my neck and pulling off my shirt. His large hands are gentle and careful as they unhook my bra and toss it on the floor.

I don't even consider feeling exposed, don't even take a moment to fear that he doesn't like what he sees. I can't. The way Michael looks at me, it's like he's kneeling at the altar of his favorite goddess. Like every part of me was made divinely perfect, and no one sees this more than him.

Softly...achingly slowly... he drags his lips down my chest and belly. Unbuttoning my jeans, he pushes them down my hips and calves. I'm on fire, responding to his every touch with sighs and gasps.

How have I gone through life without this? How have I ever known happiness without this man's touch?

Pulling my panties off, he kisses the sensitive skin on the inside of my thigh. My legs open to him, my body and heart silently begging him to do as he pleases.

His tongue is slow and cautious, testing the waters. My

hand finds his wind-tossed hair, fingers twisting through the soft locks as he licks and teases. Waves of pleasure lift me up... up...each one taking me a little higher than the last.

I buck my hips against his face, dig my nails into his scalp. I'm tossed into the very sky, the tsunami of pleasure bringing me down with a deafening crash. I'm dimly aware of someone crying out his name—I guess it must be me?—and then I'm blinking my eyes back into focus, trying to make sense of the reality-shattering experience.

There's no logic here, though. No explanation. There's only me, and there's him—me and him together, joined into one perfect rhythm.

Michael's lips find mine again, but I need more. I claw at his shirt, and he chuckles at my desperation, the throaty laugh only making me more eager to explore his body.

Pulling back, he helps me with his clothes. With each layer that falls on the floor, my jaw drops a little lower.

I knew he was fit and he was sexy... But, damn. I'm shocked I'm not blinded by the tight lines of muscles running all over his torso, arms, and legs.

Climbing back onto the bed, he pulls me to him so that I'm right on his lap. We're both naked, his dick pulsing against my inner thigh.

"I've been dreaming of this." He rakes his fingers through my hair.

"Me too," I whisper, enjoying the heat gathering between us.

"I...have condoms." He licks his lips. "And I got them for this, for whenever we found ourselves here. I didn't get them for anyone else," he hurries to explain.

"Okay." I laugh a little bit, though I'm secretly thrilled to hear that because it means he hasn't been with another woman lately. And it's not like that would cheapen our experience, but of course it's nice to hear.

That makes me feel special. It makes us special.

"Yeah." His warm breath tickles my cheek. "I just wanted you to know that."

"So…" I bite my lip and reach between us, my hand finding his throbbing length like a moth to a flame. "Are you going to get one?"

He groans in delight and nips my neck. "Yes," he rasps.

Gently setting me on the bed, he digs in his wallet. My heart picks up, and a bit of anxiety returns. It's been so long, maybe I'm out of practice…

But, no. That's not what's scaring me. It's the vulnerability of this moment. The step that means that, from now on, there are greater heights to fall from.

There's more to lose.

Once we do this, my heart will be in this game on a whole new level.

But then Michael sits on the edge of the bed, cups my face, and looks deep into my eyes. Nothing is said, but there doesn't need to be a single word. He knows how special this moment is, and we have each other to hold on to.

No one will be tumbling away, crashing to the ground.

His lips collide with mine, and this kiss is hungry and electric. He climbs over me like a lazy wave, and we sink into the mattress. Our fingers laced, he enters slowly.

Pleasure ripples through me as he stretches me open. Even in the dimly lit room, everything seems vibrant. The shadows dance, and the air is sweeter than it's ever been.

Michael kisses my lips. My chin. My throat. We rock together slowly but surely, not in a rush to get anywhere. No one has ever been this gentle with me, and it makes me open up even more.

Pressing my hands flat against his back, I draw him tighter to me. There's no such thing as close enough, and I long for his every inch to be pressed to mine. Sweat collects between us, a cocktail of our heat and lust. Pulling his lower lip into my mouth, I gently suck it between my lips, then bite down lightly with my teeth while running my nails up and down his back.

Pleasure spins up my core in a spiral. Still, he goes slowly, taking his time—so much that I might go mad. Desperate gasps slip from my lips, and he swallows them with each kiss.

Suddenly, I explode, my soul bursting from my body to be reconstructed in the ether. Michael groans into my ear, the most primal, ecstatic sound I've ever heard, and—together—we reach a new bliss.

Closing my eyes, I breathe him in. He's still above me, one hand cradling my ass and his face buried in my hair. It's the most perfect moment; if only I could bottle it up to sip from whenever I feel anything close to sad.

"You okay?" Lifting his face, he gazes at me.

The question makes me laugh. "I'm so much better than okay."

He unleashes that lopsided grin that's both boyish and masculine at the same time. "I was worried about hurting you. I didn't know if you were...having any symptoms, you know."

"No." I shake my head, touched by his concern. "You didn't hurt me."

He adjusts so that he's lying next to me on his side, the two of us face-to-face. "Good." He trails a finger down my arm.

I sigh happily. "I feel like I should say something, but... I'm at a loss for words right now."

"Me too," he chuckles.

And so we just stay where we are, the minutes ticking by, the outside world not mattering one bit.

"You know..." He runs his palm up my leg. "Katie is going

straight to school from her sleepover tomorrow, so I don't need to go anywhere. Technically, I don't need to go until you kick me out."

My stomach dances with excitement. His staying over is exactly what I want, but I was trying not to make any assumptions. "You mean you can sleep over here?"

He studies me. "As long as you'd like that. I don't want to impose—"

I shake my head. "Michael. I..." Screw it. Why am I beating around the bush? "I want you to stay."

"Good." He tugs me closer. "Because, guess what?"

"What?" I breathe as I sink into him.

"I'm crazy about you," he whispers into my ear.

And there it is. The happiest moment of my life so far.

## Chapter Fifteen

HANNAH

"There she is!" Aunt Carol's voice booms across Knit Happens, the shop door clanging shut behind her.

She leaves her suitcase by the door and walks across the store with open arms, bangles sliding on her wrists, and her curly gray hair in a high bun.

"Carol." I open my arms and step into her hug, embracing the smells of home. Her lavender body lotion. The palo santo incense that faintly clings to her clothes.

"How are you?" She steps back and studies me. "There are bags under your eyes."

"There are?" I touch my face. "Oh. I guess I'm a little tired. I didn't sleep much last night."

She frowns. "Stress?"

"Yeah," I lie, choosing not to share that it was actually the firefighter in my bed keeping me awake.

"Poor girl." She whirls around, inspecting the shop. "It looks great in here. So colorful."

"Thanks." My chest swells with pride. Knit Happens has come a long way since it was just the empty storefront Carol came to check out while I was back in Portland having a killer flare.

"What can I do?" She claps her hands together.

"Nothing," I laugh. "You just got here. Go to the house and take it easy. Unpack."

She frowns slightly. "Well, what are you doing?"

"I'm about to set up for tonight's crochet class."

Her frown deepens. "Another class? Hannah, don't you think that's too much?"

"No." I turn away from her and put up my laptop, which I was using for inventory, and try not to be annoyed.

The last week has been wonderfully good—my symptoms have been minimal, Michael and I have had lunch together every day during the week, and I have a new class, Beginner's Crocheting, which starts tonight.

It's been cloud nine for days, like almost nothing could bring me down at this point.

And I really, really want to keep that good feeling going.

"You could vacuum." I turn back to her, knowing giving her a task will keep her happy. "That would be helpful."

"Show me the way to the broom closet." She nods confidently.

We get to work cleaning and setting up for class, catching each other up on the smaller details of life as we do so. While we talk at least a couple times a week, I haven't told her much about the island. Mostly because I haven't experienced it much.

"The bird sanctuary is supposed to be really nice," I say as I fluff pillows.

Maybe Michael would like to go there sometime with me?

I smile to myself, recalling our parting kiss after lunch yesterday. We won't get to see each other as often with my aunt visiting, but maybe that's for the best. I don't want to rush things and end up screwing it all up somehow.

"Do you have any flameless candles?" Carol asks. "That would add a nice touch."

I'm about to answer when the front door opens again, and I look up in confusion. Beginner's Crochet doesn't start for another twenty minutes, and the sign is flipped to "Closed"—

I halt in the doorway, my stomach doing a somersault.

Because Michael and Katie stand on the rug, looking around. Michael seems slightly uncomfortable, his hands in his pockets and shoulders hunched up.

"Hey." My heart races.

"Hi!" Katie bounces over to me. "My dad and I are here for the crochet class."

I feel my eyebrows rise. "You are?" I ask Michael. "I didn't know you were into crafting."

He shrugs. "Katie told me crocheting is easier than knitting, and I need a new hobby. Working on the fire station kitchen is stressing me out."

Katie nods sagely and turns to me. "And you said crafting is a great way of shutting your brain off and being mindful."

"That's right," I murmur. "I did say that."

Carol lightly clears her throat, reminding me that she's even here.

"Michael, Katie," I say, "this is my aunt, Carol."

Carol advances on Michael, hand out and gaze sharp. "It's so good to meet you."

"You too," he says warmly, shaking her hand. He turns to me. "I hope we're not too early. We can go to the coffee shop..."

"No," I nearly shout. "Please stay. And it's great you both are here. Katie, do you want to go pick out your supplies for the class? They're in the baskets over there."

"I'll come with you, Katie." Carol's love for kids emerges. "I need to pick out some for myself. What color do you think goes well with purple and blue?"

As soon as they're on the other side of the room, Michael steps closer to me and lowers his voice. "Is this all right?"

It takes me a moment to answer, I'm so distracted by his close proximity. "Of course."

"I just didn't know how you would feel about Katie being... here...seeing us together."

I blink at him. "That's your call."

His lips twitch into a soft smile. "She wanted to come to this class. Plus, I wanted to see you."

"So, you're not really interested in crocheting?" I chuckle, already knowing the answer.

He smirks. "Guilty as charged."

I bite into my smile and put my hands in my jeans pockets so that I don't reach out for him. My skin is itching to be pressed against his, and longing spirals through me. Though we've been able to steal moments together during the day, we haven't had an evening together since that night at my house, and I've been aching for more.

"I found mine," Katie calls across the room. "Dad, what color crochet hooks do you want?"

Our moment is over—for now.

Stepping away from Michael, I busy myself with prepping for the class, though thoughts of his lips and hands all over my body never leave my mind. It's good that we each have our own lives, and he has Katie, of course, but sometimes I wish we could steal away to a private island and spend weeks naked in a hut, just the two of us.

The rest of the class filters in, bringing the group to a nice head count of eight. I go over the project that we'll be working on, making sure I don't look at Michael too much while I speak. Once everyone gets to work, I go around the room giving one-on-one guidance.

Katie is a natural, and the others are doing a pretty good

job, too. Plus, there's my aunt, who was the person who first taught me to crochet and knit, outshining everyone. She might as well be teaching the class herself. There's only one person who's struggling.

"Here. Can I demonstrate?" I crouch and hold out my hands.

"Please." Michael hands me his crochet hooks, but instead, I place my hands over top of his to guide him.

The simple touch ignites a fire that roars in my core. I guide Michael's hands through the chain stitch, but more than once, I feel his gaze on my face instead of the project.

"Does that clear it up?" Hard as it is, I let go of him.

He gazes at me. "Sure."

I have to bite back a laugh. He's clearly more interested in me than the project. But what about Katie? Even an eleven-year-old could notice this chemistry.

She's distracted, though, chatting away with the town's mayor while they crochet. Which makes me relax at least a little bit.

I'm not sure what I'm afraid of more—Katie not liking that her dad and I are dating, or her loving it and then being crushed if the two of us don't work out.

And what are Michael's thoughts on it? I can't get a clear read. Does he want me to act like we're nothing more than friends, or is he waiting for me to make the first move and show him some affection in front of his daughter?

It's all so confusing. If only we'd had a briefing before the two of them showed up together.

Not that I'm unhappy to see them—I'm thrilled. Katie is awesome, and I'm completely smitten with her dad. It's unanswered questions that I have a challenging time with.

The class ends too soon, but to my delight, Michael and Katie don't leave with the others.

"Can we help you clean up?" Michael is already helping Carol stack the chairs and cushions, so it looks like he won't take no for an answer anyway.

"Sure. Thank you." I gather the supplies into their baskets.

"Can you two come to pizza with us?" Katie flops down on a cushion that her dad was just about to pick up. "Every week, we go to this pizza place on the mainland. They make cheeseburger pizza, and it's sooo good. Get Stuffed won't serve it, even though I've asked the owner, like, twelve times. I even put it in my last letter to Santa, but the most I ever got here was a cheese slice with pickles on it." She sticks out her tongue.

"Oh, I don't know…" I trail off and glance at my aunt.

She touches my shoulder. "I need to get to the house and unpack, but you should go."

"No," I say quickly. "I'll come home with you."

She squeezes her shoulder. "Go, Hannah. We'll have plenty of time together later. Plus, I grabbed something at the airport. I'm not hungry."

I cut my gaze to Michael. What does he want?

He's watching me, though—trying to get a read—and I can't take all the uncertainty anymore.

"I would love it if Hannah went," Michael says, "but she might be too tired—"

"Count me in," I blurt out.

His mouth drops in shock, but a moment later, he's smiling, eyes sparkling. "Great."

Carol's smile is soft. "Does this place have anything other than pizza?"

"Oh. Uh." He frowns, clearly thinking. "Yeah. They do."

"You should get a salad," she tells me. "Or gluten-free, if they have it. The gluten could be sapping your energy."

"Maybe," I mumble. "Do you remember where the key is?"

"Yes." She gives me a quick hug. "I'll be fine. You go have fun. And remember, gluten!"

"Okay." I give her a grateful smile, though a part of me wishes she were coming with. Doing something unexpected would feel better with her by my side.

She grabs her suitcase. "Good to meet you both," she tells Michael and Katie.

"You too." Michael opens the door for her, and I lean to watch her through the window as she gets into her rental car.

"Ready to go?" Katie asks, bouncing from foot to foot.

"Yep. Thanks for inviting me," I say, surprised with myself for doing something that hasn't been planned at least twenty-four hours in advance.

I don't usually do anything spontaneous. I like to know what's coming next, because that helps keep my fibro and anxiety in check. But maybe I'm changing.

Maybe I'm starting to feel safe around Michael.

Grabbing my coat, I cast him a long, soft look. He opens the door, letting Katie go first. As I step through, he grazes my waist with his hand, and pure ecstasy shoots through me.

Maybe I'm more than feeling safe around him, I realize as I lock the door and the three of us walk down the street. Maybe I'm starting to *trust* him.

Me. After years of trusting only a select few people—and certainly no men. But here I am, a flower opening up, turning its petals to the sun that is Michael Greer.

# *Chapter Sixteen*

MICHAEL

The mainland is like a whole different world. Here, no one knows who I am—unless it's one of the occasional instances when I'll bump into someone from the island. People are doing their thing, rushing to work or their next errand, and not one of them gives a damn about who I am or what I'm doing.

I can just be. And tonight, I can do that with Hannah by my side.

The drive over the bridge and into town is upbeat, Katie dominating the conversation with news from school. If Hannah is bored, it doesn't show; from all appearances, she's hanging on every word about who might have put the graffiti in the girls' bathroom and the argument over whether the next dance's theme should be "Winter Wonderland" or "'90s Nostalgia."

"I don't know if this place has gluten-free pizza," I say when there's a break in the conversation.

Hannah shakes her head. "That doesn't matter. Carol has a lot of...opinions about what I should and shouldn't eat. I already know gluten isn't a trigger for me."

"Does she know that?" I cock an eyebrow.

Hannah looks out the window. "I've told her."

Her voice is suddenly smaller, her shoulders hunched over. Maybe I shouldn't have mentioned her aunt.

It's strange, though. Hannah seemed genuinely excited about Carol coming to visit. Watching them together, though, I sensed some tension.

Maybe that's just the way it is with family, though. God knows my mom and I don't have a perfect relationship by any means.

Parking on the street, we walk down the block to the pizza place Katie and I hit up every week. My hand aches to slip into Hannah's, but I hold back. Is Katie ready for that?

I know I am.

In the short time since Hannah and I have started dating, my opinion on keeping things from my daughter has changed. Jenny was right; Katie can handle a lot more than I was giving her credit for.

I like this woman—a lot—and why not show Katie what healthy dating looks like? Plus, Katie seems to like Hannah.

I just need to make absolutely sure. I need to talk to Katie about it before I go any further, need to see where her head is at.

The two of them walk ahead of me, laughing over some knitting joke Hannah just shared. My lips pull into a smile, but at the same time, my chest aches.

My dad was right, as much as I hate to admit it. Aside from the annual visit to Pine Island, Katie didn't have any female influences growing up. At eleven, it seems that I've robbed her of years of important interactions.

Is it too late? Have I fucked up that part of parenting completely?

We arrive at the pizza joint, and Katie slides into the booth next to Hannah, stealing any opportunity for my leg to rub against Hannah's under the table.

Oh well. At least sitting across from her means I can look at her.

And, damn. She looks gorgeous tonight. Her blonde hair has a slight wave in it, highlighting the mix of white and light-blonde strands I hadn't noticed before. Instead of the glasses she often wears at work, she's opted for contacts, I assume, causing her blue eyes to really stand out. And the all-black outfit makes her look like a beat poet about to take the stage.

"Dad. You're staring."

"Huh?" I blink at Katie.

She snorts. "You were staring at Hannah."

My face warms. Shit. How do I even answer that?

"It's okay." Katie leans back in the booth, a knowing look on her face. "You can stare at your girlfriend. It's allowed. It's just funny, is all. You had a goofy look. Like this." She demonstrates, dropping her jaw and crossing her eyes.

Hannah presses her fingers to her lips, but it does little to stifle her laugh. Meanwhile, my mental gears are turning so fast they're probably overheating.

I haven't called Hannah my girlfriend. Ever. But hell yeah, I would love to give her that title... If she'll take it.

I try to catch her gaze, but she's looking at someone approaching the table.

"Hey, guys. How are you doing?" The waitress puts down some water glasses and then cocks her head at me. "Michael?"

Oh no. Someone from Pine Island works here?

I force a smile, trying to place her. Brunette...about thirty... green eyes...

Nope. It does nothing for me.

"Rochelle," she supplies.

With that, the memory hits me. A dark bar on the mainland. Last call. Following Rochelle's car back to her place. A frenzied, drunk couple of hours, followed by my leaving in the middle of the night without asking for her number.

That was, what? Four years ago?

Okay, yes. So, I've engaged in random hookups from time to time. They haven't been my proudest moments, and there's a reason I always left the island to find someone. I didn't want to bring any part of that habit into my regular life.

But now it looks as if I've done exactly that.

"How...are you?" Something feels stuck in my throat—air?—and I cough.

"Good." She gives me a quick eyebrow raise, the daggers from her eyes piercing me right in the face.

"You're our waitress?" I ask, aware of Katie and Hannah looking at me.

"I'm the owner. I was just bringing your waters over. Your waitress will be here soon. Enjoy dinner." She smiles at Hannah and Katie before turning on her heel and striding away.

I pick up the menu and hide my face behind it. "What are we having tonight?"

"Cheeseburger pizza. Of course. Why are you acting so weird?" Katie gets up. "Whatever. Tell me later. I need to go to the bathroom."

"What do you mean?" I guffaw. "I'm not being weird."

But she's already gone. Which means it's just Hannah and me, and for the first time, I'm not thrilled about it.

She frowns at me from across the table. "What's wrong?"

"Uh..." I fiddle with my silverware. I could lie, brush off her concern.

But so far, I've been nothing but honest with her, and I'd really like to keep that habit going.

"The owner...Rochelle... We have a bit of a past."

Her brow furrows slightly. "You dated?"

Shit. "Not...dated." I rub the spot between my eyebrows,

wishing my seat would open up and swallow me whole. "We had one night together. After meeting at a bar."

"Oh. Okay. And you haven't seen her in a while?"

"She wasn't the only one," I go on. Might as well get it all out there while we're on the subject. "Not that I did it all the time, but when Katie and I came back to visit while we lived in Seattle, it would be my only time on my own, and I..."

"You found women to hook up with."

I cringe. "Yeah."

Shit. Is she going to hate me now? See me as some sort of sick, weird creep?

Or, even worse, think that I'm only using her for sex?

"I get it," she says, taking me by surprise.

"You do?"

She shrugs once. "Yeah. It makes sense that you would use your few hours off from being a dad to have an...adult night with someone."

"Yeah." I nod, but the topic still feels incomplete. "I wanted more. I just...wouldn't allow myself to go searching for it. Until you."

"Oh. Really?" Her voice is silky, making me want to reach across the table and pull her into my lap.

"Yeah," I breathe. "Hannah..."

"The pizza's not here?" Katie interrupts, taking her seat next to Hannah.

"We haven't even ordered it yet," Hannah laughs.

The rest of the dinner is smooth—perfect. Katie and I share all the best sledding spots on the island come winter, and Hannah tells us all about the grant she's applying for.

As we're walking to my truck after dessert at the ice cream shop on the corner, Katie slips her hand into Hannah's. "Can you stay over for a sleepover tonight?"

I suck in a sharp breath. One, it's a school night. Two,

Hannah is an adult who probably doesn't want to make a fort and braid hair with an eleven-year-old. Three, her aunt is in town, and she needs to go home to her. And four...

I hope that Hannah says yes anyway.

Because I'd really like for her to sleep over—in my room.

But can Katie handle that? What will she think, knowing I have a woman in there? Will it make her too attached too quickly to Hannah?

"Ooh." Hannah swings Katie's hand back and forth. "That sounds like so much fun, but I have an early morning staff meeting with Flick."

"Aw." Katie pouts. "Can we do it soon?"

"Your dad and I can talk about it."

Katie shoots me a look over her shoulder, a silent plea for me to agree.

"We'll talk about it," I echo.

We climb into the truck, and Katie puts on the latest pop hits to sing along to as we drive Hannah home.

"We'll have a sleepover soon?" Katie asks as we pull into Hannah's driveway.

"Soon," she says with a smile.

"I'll walk you to your door. Be right back, Katie." I get out of the truck before Katie demands an explanation as to why Hannah can't get inside herself—though maybe she understands I want a moment alone with her.

"Thank you for dinner." Hannah steps to the side of the porch, where it curves around the house, out of Katie's sight.

"Thank you for coming along." I wrap my arms around her waist and tug her close. "Hey... I would love for you to come over for a sleepover."

Her eyes search my face. "Yeah? In that case, it's a promise. We'll have a sleepover. Soon."

Lowering my head, I kiss her gently. Shivers run down my spine, and my hands ache to explore her body, but I step back.

Another time. Soon.

A curtain moves in the front window, and I frown. Was Carol watching us?

"What?" Hannah follows my gaze to the window.

"Nothing." I smooth my hand down her cheek. "I can't wait to see you again."

"Same," she breathes.

"Good night." I leave her house grinning and climb into my truck.

Did she really mean that? Is she comfortable enough to stay at my house? And with both me and Katie?

Am I comfortable with it?

As I back out of the driveway, I realize that I am. I'm more than comfortable with it. I'm craving it, and so much more, from Hannah. I'm ready for the next steps, and it doesn't matter that I don't know exactly what those are.

I'll be taking them with her, and that's enough for me.

## *Chapter Seventeen*

HANNAH

"There was so much there. You would have loved it," Flick gushes. "Look at this one."

She pulls another yarn sample from her bag, and I run my fingers over the silky coil. "Beautiful," I murmur.

"Next year." She smiles at me across Knit Happens's counter.

"Next year," I confirm, though I'm really not that disappointed I had to miss the yarn convention. Even though I couldn't take off from the shop, there's so much good happening in my life—my classes taking off, my relationship with Michael blooming—that I haven't even been thinking about what I've been missing out on.

"Did anything happen while I was gone?" Flick sets her folded arms on the counter and leans into them.

"Not much. The new classes went well...and I went out for pizza the other night with Michael and Katie."

Her eyes go round. "You did? Hannah, that's huge!"

"Is it?" I ask, though I've suspected it is, and I'm relieved to hear she agrees.

"Michael doesn't strike me as the kind of person who

would let just anyone around his kid. He seems too protective for that."

"Yeah," I murmur. "I think so too."

"How was it?"

"Really nice. Katie is cool. I like her a lot."

"Oh my God, this is so adorable."

My phone beeps with a text. "That's him now."

"Of course it is. Is he sending you kissy emojis?"

"No." Laughing, I read the text—and enjoy the warmth that washes through me. "He invited me and Carol over to dinner tonight. With him and Katie."

I put the phone down, a little shook. "I've never been to his house before."

"Another big step. He must really like you."

My tummy churns with excitement and anxiety. "Yeah..."

Picking up my phone again, I call Carol, who is at the grocery store grabbing us some things for the week.

"Hey," I say right when she answers. "Whatever you're grabbing for dinner right now, pause. Michael invited us to have dinner with him and Katie."

"That's so sweet of him," Carol coos. "But you'll be so tired after work. I planned on having dinner ready so you can just sit on the couch and relax."

"Oh. That's nice of you." I hesitate, not wanting to offend her. "I'm feeling good, though, and I'd like to go to their house. With you."

She makes that popping sound with her lips that says she's thinking hard. "O...kay. I suppose there's no harm in saying yes, and then if you need to cancel, you—"

"I won't need to cancel. I'll be fine."

"We'll see when the time comes. When are we going?"

"Dinner's at seven thirty." I grit my teeth. Why does it feel like she's trying to sabotage the night?

"And you'll be home before then? So that you can rest? I'll come cover at the shop if you need me to."

"I have the Chronic Pain Crafters meetup tonight, so I'll just have time to come home and grab you."

"Hannah—"

"I'll be fine." I rush through my words, not giving her a chance to argue.

"I just— Look, Hannah. I've been meaning to talk to you about this."

"What do you mean?" I step away from the counter, arms folded tight over my chest.

"I'm concerned you're moving too fast with Michael."

My jaw drops, the sting more than I expected. How can she say that? "What do you mean?"

"He has a child. Katie is wonderful—it's not that I think there's anything wrong with her or her father. They're both great. I just want to make sure you take your time, that you don't rush into something you're not ready for."

My face burns, and I stare out the window, vision blurring. "We're just dating. It's not like we're getting married."

"I know, but it's different when there's a child involved."

"I know that."

"Do you? Because I really don't think you can, not until you become a parent yourself. Are you ready to step into that role?"

"I..." I open and close my mouth, at a loss for words. Michael isn't asking me to step in as Katie's mother. We just started dating.

Though to be fair, the idea of doing that doesn't scare me. I've always wanted kids, and Carol knows that. So what is this really about?

"You think I wouldn't be a good parent because of the

fibromyalgia." I wipe away the tears that have started trickling down my cheeks.

"No, Hannah. I know you would be a great parent. I know from personal experience how exhausting parenting is, though."

"So, what? I should just never do it? Because that's the only option. Fibromyalgia isn't going anywhere." My voice is rising, and I hate it. Thank God it's only Flick in the shop.

"No. Don't twist my words."

"Be more careful with your words," I snap. "And if you don't want to come to dinner tonight, don't. No one is making you."

The line becomes quiet, and in the silence, I feel the last of my good mood withering.

"I didn't mean to insult you," my aunt says quietly. "That was never my intention."

"I know." I sigh. "And I'm sorry. I overreacted."

"I would love to join the three of you for dinner tonight."

"Okay. I'll see you at seven." Feeling exhausted, I hang up.

"Everything okay?" Flick asks.

"Yeah. She's worried about me." Blinking back the rest of my tears, I rejoin her at the counter.

"What else is new?"

"It's just a little harder to deal with when she's not three thousand miles away." I text Michael back, telling him we'll be there at seven thirty and asking if I can bring anything.

It feels kind of weird that Michael has been to my house but I've never been to his, although I get it. His home is a space that he shares with Katie; bringing me there also means bringing me into her world.

Is it the success of our pizza dinner the other night that has spurred this invitation? And am I ready to step into Katie's world?

And is my aunt right? Would being a part of Katie's life be more than I can handle?

Even though I'm just the woman dating her father, I know being in a kid's life to even the smallest degree comes with a great amount of responsibility. I'm up for the challenge, for sure. I just want to make sure I don't screw it up.

It hurts that my aunt even suggested I could do that. Like I'm not taking my entry into Katie's world seriously.

Carol is acting like she doesn't even know me. Like I've just been skipping through life, making snap decisions, never considering the repercussions.

If she were to really stop and think, she would remember that's the opposite of me. I never take action unless I know for sure that it's the right thing to do.

"I need to cool down," I huff to Flick.

She's watching me with a wary look. "Yeah, I've never seen you this worked up after talking to her. Are you sure it's a good idea to have her visit for this long?"

I don't even know how to answer that, and I don't have to.

The door opens, and in walks Jenny with a gray-haired woman. Heat climbs into my face. I don't know why, but it's embarrassing that Flick and I were just talking about her brother and niece, and I'm almost worried she somehow knows.

"Hi!" Jenny goes right for the skein she wants, grabs it, and brings it to the counter. "How's it going? Hannah, Flick, this is my mother, Cynthia."

My heart leaps into my throat. Michael's mom?

I want to pat my hair and make sure it's not the mess I suspect it is, but I stay frozen behind the counter. "H-hello."

"It's nice to meet you." Cynthia smiles at us both.

"You must be working some kind of magic," Jenny says to me, shaking her head in delight. "Because Michael has been walking around with a shit-eating grin for days."

I bite my lip. Oh. So, we're doing this. Right in front of Cynthia.

But it seems that Jenny's mom picks up on my discomfort. "Jenny, leave the poor girl alone. She doesn't have to explain herself."

I smile at her in gratitude, liking her already.

Over her shoulder, Devin, Maya, and Alexis enter the shop. Is it six already? How did the day go by so quickly?

"It was nice to meet you, Cynthia. I should go set up for my crafting group."

Relieved that Flick is ringing Jenny up, I sidle out from behind the counter and hurry to the center of the room. "Hey, guys."

"Hey." Alexis's mouth draws thin.

I freeze. "What's wrong?"

Her gaze cuts to Maya, who looks pale and unsteady.

"Maya?" My breath catches. "You okay?"

"I'm fine." Her smile is clearly forced. "I'm not feeling great, but I wanted to come anyway."

"Are you sure?" Alexis asks. "It's not too late to—"

"Absolutely." Taking a seat, Maya opens her bag and pulls out her knitting project.

"Bye, Hannah!" Jenny calls as she and her mom leave. I give them a quick wave before turning back to Maya—who seems determined not to meet my gaze.

"Hey." Flick joins us in the circle. "What are we working on tonight?"

Devin pulls out the scarf she started the other day. "I want to finish this for the firefighter's fundraiser."

"Ooh, right. I have to finish my stuff for it too."

The five of us settle in and get to work, the conversation turning to the Makers Market on the mainland next month.

Although Maya isn't exactly a chatty person, she talks less than usual, and twenty minutes into the night, her head is hanging.

I bite the inside of my cheek, knowing there's little I can do. If Maya's lupus is acting up but she still wants to go about her daily life, there's nothing that I or any of us can say to convince her otherwise.

And so I hold back and don't bring up her health, though that doesn't stop me from regularly glancing at her to make sure she's okay.

"When does the farmers market start?" Devin asks.

"April." Flick holds up her finished hat and studies it with satisfaction. "And it goes through October."

Maya fidgets in her chair, the bottom of her legging riding up and exposing an ankle so swollen I gasp. "Maya," I say.

"Hmm?" She looks at me with a distant expression, her eyebrows pinched.

I put down my knitting. Screw biting my tongue. I'm not an expert in lupus, but I know that what's happening right now can't be good.

"Your ankle..." I swallow. "Let's get you home."

Alexis has also stopped what she's doing to observe Maya's ankle. "No, we need to get you to the hospital."

My heart beats faster. Alexis and Maya have known each other for the longest of anyone in this group, so if anyone knows about Maya's flares, it has to be Alexis. If she says Maya needs to be at the hospital, well then, we're going to the hospital.

"I'm...fine," Maya squeaks out.

Flick sighs. "Oh, sweetie, you could barely finish that sentence. I'll pull my car around front."

She jogs out of the building, and Devin, Alexis, and I help Maya to the door. She walks like a robot, shuffling along, and by the time we reach the front door, she's stopped trying to convince us she's all right.

Flick's car idles at the curb, and Alexis and I hold on to Maya's arms as she walks to it.

"How are you doing?" Alexis asks.

"I'm... I'm..." Maya's head rolls to the side, her eyes shut, and she goes limp in our arms.

"Maya." Alexis's voice pitches. "Maya!"

But she won't open her eyes, won't give any indication that she's even still in this world.

# *Chapter Eighteen*

MICHAEL

"**I**s this small enough?" Katie stops chopping and turns to me.

I have to bite back a laugh; the bell pepper pieces are so micro you can barely see them. Is it possible that she's even more nervous about Hannah and her aunt coming to dinner than I am?

Maybe, but there's no way she's as excited as I am.

"I'm going to wash the windows." She steps away from the cutting board and opens the closet with the cleaning supplies.

"You already washed them."

"The front ones might be dirty again."

Apparently, I spoke too soon. She just might be more excited than me.

Which has me thinking.

How does Katie see Hannah? Is she only a cool and pretty adult to hang out with, or is she more than that? Does Katie see the potential there that I do?

They're questions that have me wondering other things. Like if Katie has been craving a mother all these years and hasn't mentioned it because she doesn't want to hurt me. Or if she hasn't mentioned it because she's figured there's no point. I haven't dated, and from what she's seen, I haven't shown any interest in women. Maybe she assumed that I didn't want to find a partner and left it at that.

The realization gives me instant acid reflux.

I kept women out of my life for years because I didn't want a repeat of what happened with Talia, but was that a mistake? Did I end up hurting my daughter more than helping her?

The shrieking of the smoke alarm pierces my thoughts, and I rush over to the oven and pull out the potatoes. Luckily, only a few pieces are burned.

"Hello!" a familiar voice rings through the house.

I turn from the oven as my mother walks into the kitchen. "Hi. Did you... I didn't hear you knock."

"Oh, Michael. Katie let me in. You know I wouldn't just walk into your house."

No. I don't know that.

"What's up?" I open a window and fan the smoke in its direction, hoping to prevent the smoke alarm from going off again.

"Well...I met Hannah." Her lips curl into a knowing smile. "She's pretty."

"She's more than that." My heart skips a beat. How much longer till she arrives for dinner?

I glance at the clock. Thirty minutes. Thirty minutes too long.

"...at the town meeting yesterday," my mom is saying.

"Huh?" I turn back to her. "Sorry. What was that?"

"I saw Pat at the town meeting." She starts folding my dish towels that are strewn around the kitchen. "He's worried that you're completely ignoring your father's plans for the firehouse kitchen."

"Mom." I stare at her, hoping that alone will be enough to end this conversation.

But apparently it won't be. "I'm serious. He's not happy about this."

"It's not his project," I sigh. "He doesn't need to be happy about it."

"Just hear him out." Finished with the dish towels, she moves on to inspecting my fridge. "You've had this ketchup for months."

"It's good for months." I cross my arms over my chest.

She closes the fridge. "He's been in this business for years, and he's helped half the town remodel their businesses at one time or another."

I cock an eyebrow. Surely she knows she's exaggerating.

But maybe she doesn't care. She just wants me to do things her way, like everyone else—or, more specifically, my dad's way. Saint Ted Greer.

"You know, Mom, I did run my own contracting business for years, and I've worked in fire stations for even longer. I'm pretty sure I know more about what the fire station needs than Pat does."

This isn't about what Pat thinks. It's about what my dad thought. But it doesn't matter. Either way, I won't be caving. I know what I'm doing, even if no one in this damn town agrees.

She purses her lips and shakes her head. "You are being so defensive and hardheaded."

I freeze, her words a knife to my gut. Those are the two things my dad always accused me of being. It's like she's pulled the labels out of the dusty drawer just to hurt me.

My hands curl into fists, and my exhale burns my nostrils. "Have a good night, Mom."

Because I can't stand to look at her a moment longer, I stalk out the back door and onto the porch. My shoes beat a heavy rhythm across the wooden planks, back and forth as I try to calm down.

How could she even think of saying that to me? Does she not see how hard I'm working every single day? Does the fact that I moved Katie here and took up Dad's torch at the fire station not mean anything to her?

My phone rings in my pocket, and I pull it out. Hannah's name flashing across the screen is a cool balm to my heart.

"Hey," I answer.

"Hi." Her voice is strained, and there's chatter in the background.

I frown. "Everything okay?"

"I'm at the hospital with my crafting group. I'm sorry, we won't be able to make it to dinner tonight."

I clutch the phone, panic taking hold. "The hospital? Are you okay? What happened?"

"Yeah, I'm fine. It's Maya. Her lupus. She'll be okay, but we're all going to stay here."

I blow out a breath. Poor Maya. I only talked to her that one time at school, but she's obviously a sweet woman. Anything less than amazing things happening to her is a travesty.

"It's okay," I tell her. "You be with your friend. She's lucky to have people like you all."

"Thank you." She sighs. "I really am sad that I have to miss dinner."

"I know," I say softly. "I'm bummed about it too. Let me know if you need anything while you're there."

"I will. Thanks, Michael."

My name flowing from her lips is nearly enough to make me forget why I even came out to this porch in the first place. "You're welcome. Talk soon."

We hang up, and I take a seat in the wicker rocking chair. There go my plans for tonight. Now what will Katie and I do with all this food? I overestimated servings when I went shopping, and we have enough to feed a baseball team.

Maybe I'll freeze it for quick meals during the week, and the two of us can grab some cheeseburger pizza. Without Hannah coming over, I'm now in the mood to get off the island anyway.

The back door opens, and Katie pokes her head out. "Grandma said goodbye."

My lips blow out with an exhale. Of course she did, and that makes me look like even more of an asshole after kicking her out.

"When's Hannah getting here?" Katie asks.

"Actually, honey, something happened to...her friend." I don't want to tell Katie it's her art teacher. That would be too upsetting.

"Which friend?"

I press my tongue against my front teeth. What am I doing? She can handle this truth.

"Your teacher Maya. Don't worry, though. Hannah says she's okay. Hannah and her friends are going to spend the evening at the hospital so that Maya isn't lonely."

"Oh." She blinks in concern. "Okay. We should take them dinner."

Of course we should. Why didn't I think of that?

"Honey, that's a great idea." Standing, I kiss the top of her head. "Let's go pack it up."

From the other end of the house, I hear the sound of the front door opening. "I forgot my purse," my mom calls out.

Maya's eyes light up. "I'll invite Grandma."

Before I can respond, she's off at the speed of light, running into the house. I close my eyes and shake my head.

Great. So, this has turned into a family outing. An affair that should be private but is now everyone else's business. Just like everything else on this island.

Why should I be surprised?

# Chapter Nineteen

HANNAH

Sitting back down on the hard waiting room chair, I pick up my knitting needles—Devin was kind enough to run back to the shop and get our projects for us to work on while we're at the hospital—but I haven't finished two stitches before I set them back down.

It's been over an hour since we heard anything about Maya, and I'm about to crawl out of my skin.

From her spot in the corner where she's crocheting, Alexis smiles at me. The expression doesn't reach her eyes, but it's good to know that she understands how I'm feeling. We're not in this alone.

Even though we've only been a crafting group for a few weeks, it already feels like I've known these women my whole life. I can't imagine going forward without them.

Flashbacks of Maya outside Knit Happens return. The way her words slurred, her eyes closing as she went limp. We didn't know what had happened, and thank God she came to less than a minute later. According to the doctor, she'd probably passed out from pain.

I shake my head, almost wanting to laugh. People with

135

chronic pain are the toughest. We can walk around all day long, every day, smiling our way through pain that would have most people on the floor. As awful as it is, you kind of...well, not get used to it. More like learn to live with it.

Or live in spite of it.

Sighing, I spin on my heel and start pacing. It sucks that Maya thought she had to grin and bear it, but I get it—and I've been guilty of doing the same thing many times.

Which makes me wonder if I'm getting dangerously in over my head. This last week, my schedule has been jam-packed, what with classes, the shop, and finishing up my grant application. I should probably slow down, but I've been having too much fun. Especially when Michael is involved.

"Excuse me," a middle-aged woman in one of the chairs says. "What is it you girls are working on?"

I follow her gaze to Alexis, Devin, and Flick, all three of them knitting or crocheting away. "Oh. We're making some pieces for the firefighter's fundraiser. Scarves, hats, and things like that to auction off."

Her eyes brighten. "I've always wanted to knit. It looks so calming."

"Would you like to learn how to now?" I ask, not even thinking about it.

She looks surprised but nods eagerly, and the next thing I know, we're sitting side by side as I teach her to cast on. The few other people in the waiting room take notice, and I invite them over. With the needles that are in the bottom of the basket Devin grabbed, I have enough for everyone.

It's funny. When I was sitting trying to knit by myself, I couldn't get in the zone. But teaching makes me feel hyperfocused, like nothing could pull me out of the reverie that is yarn, the clicking of plastic on plastic, and the slowing down of thoughts.

Nothing except Michael, that is.

I swear I sense him come in. It's a shift in the air, like the electric charge that comes on before a big storm. Looking up, I see him striding through the automatic doors, a monolith of comfort and security.

He's not alone. Katie and Cynthia flank him, all three of them carrying canvas tote bags.

Michael's gaze sweeps the area and lands on me. I trail off, forgetting where I was in my lesson for this impromptu class, and put my needles down.

"Uh, hopefully that can get everyone started." I stand. "I'll be right back. Flick can help if you have any questions."

Skirting around the pots full of peace lilies and scheffleras, I meet the three of them by the check-in desk. "Hi. What are you doing here?" I shake my head, realizing how rude that sounded. "Not that I'm not happy to see you. Um...hi."

"We brought you dinner," Katie announces.

"Enough for everyone," Michael adds.

"You did?" My jaw drops. Talk about going the extra mile. "You didn't have to do that."

"Of course we didn't." Michael's gaze holds mine. "But we wanted to."

Tears fill my eyes, and I wish we were alone so that I could sink into his arms and show how grateful I am for him—in a way that requires privacy. And it's not just about tonight; it's about everything he's done for me since we've met.

Trekking over here with bags of food is just the cherry on top.

"Thank you," I sigh. "The cafeteria here sucks."

Cynthia chuckles. "Oh, we know."

"Hannah," Michael says. "This is my mom—"

"Cynthia," I finish. "We actually met earlier today. Thank you for coming," I tell her.

"You're welcome." She pats my shoulder. "How is your friend?"

"We, uh, don't know yet." My stomach twists. "We're still waiting to hear anything."

"Katie," Cynthia says, "help me serve dinner. Make a plate for everyone in the waiting room. We have more than enough." She takes Michael's bag from him, and she and Katie hustle over to the others.

"I'm so sorry." Michael wraps me in a hug and draws me close. I'm back in that warm, safe place that makes me melt from the inside out. Snug in his embrace, I feel like nothing could ever go wrong. I'm in a cocoon of perfection, worries vanishing like wisps of smoke.

"Thank you," I whisper into his flannel shirt. Taking a deep inhale, I step back. If I stay pressed against him any longer, I might get too relaxed and fall asleep while standing. At this point, I'm pretty sure it's only adrenaline keeping me going. "Her ankle was swollen. She passed out. I don't know if it's her lupus..."

I trail off. How much of this have I told him? Our phone call seems days ago.

A door opens, and the doctor that we saw with Maya earlier emerges. I nearly sprint to her.

"Is she okay?" I ask.

The woman smiles. "It's not lupus nephritis, which is good. It's just a run-of-the-mill kidney infection. A pretty awful one, but she'll be just fine. I'd like to keep her overnight to monitor her and then send her home in the morning."

"Thank God." My shoulders drop with the biggest sigh that's ever existed. The rest of the crafting group gathers round, asking questions. Knowing they can report back to me, I head for the bathroom.

I need to splash some water on my face. Wake myself up.

Now that I know Maya is all right and I've relaxed some, I'm even more exhausted.

"I'll be right back," I tell Michael, giving his hand a squeeze, and then dip into the women's bathroom before anyone can talk to me.

The fluorescent lights are too bright, and my skin aches. There's a pounding in my temples, and my whole head feels as heavy as a bowling ball. I just need a little refresher…just a moment to get myself together.

After splashing water on my face, I dry it with paper towels and put my glasses back on. The woman in the mirror looks absolutely drained—which is a shock.

I thought I was doing so well this week. Yes, I've been busy, but I've been managing it.

The door opens, and in the bathroom mirror, I see my aunt enter. "There you are," she says.

"Hey." Turning around, I put on a smile, but she sees right through it.

"Are you all right?" She touches my forehead.

"Fine," I lie. "And the doctor said Maya will be okay. It's a kidney infection."

She nods. "Michael told me." Her frown doesn't go anywhere. "Hannah, you need to go home and rest."

"I know. I am." With great effort, I push off from where I've been leaning against the counter.

Chewing my bottom lip, I lead the way out of the bathroom. I'll just go home and climb into bed early… Then, in the morning…

Black spots appear in front of me, and the waiting room tilts.

"Hannah!" Katie yells.

I feel her arms go around me, but she's so small, she struggles to keep me up. I reach my hand up, grabbing on to the back of a chair.

"We got you." My aunt grabs me from behind, helping Katie to hold me up.

"Hey." It's Michael's deep, calm voice. "Hannah. Sit down. Here you go."

Someone puts a chair behind me, and I comply. Everything is still blurry, and a searing ache is entering all my joints, from my shoulders to my feet.

"What do you need?" Michael crouches in front of me.

"She needs rest." Carol's voice is sharp. "She shouldn't be here. She needs to be home."

She sounds angry, but with whom, I don't know. "It's not their fault," I mumble.

"Hannah." She crouches in front of me, right next to Michael. "I'm calling a doctor to take a look at you."

Tears fill my eyes. I can't believe I'm stealing all the attention from Maya. She's the one hospitalized. "I just need to go to bed. I'm... This is a flare."

It's hard to get out, so hard to admit that I haven't been taking care of myself properly. I pushed too hard again, and the emotional stress around Maya has tipped me over the edge.

Carol's lips draw thin. "This is worse than the other ones. We're at the hospital. We can have you looked—"

"No." It takes nearly the last of my energy to get the word out.

She doesn't know what my flares have been like recently, because she hasn't been around. And, of course, that's not her fault—we live states away. I just wish she understood that this is my body, my flare. I know how to deal with it. There's nothing the hospital can do for me anyway. If they admit me and I get in to see a doctor, they'll just look at me like I'm crazy for asking to be seen when I already know how to care for myself.

"There's no point," I tell my aunt.

"Of course there is." She shakes her head, long earrings sweeping against her shoulders. "This isn't like the other ones."

"It is," Michael says. "Her last flare was like this."

Carol's face turns red. "I've known Hannah for years. If she doesn't—"

"And Hannah knows her own body." His voice is calm and collected but firm. He turns back to me. "Hannah?"

Michael touches my wrist, and I wince. It's a light touch, but it sends pain up my arm.

"Sorry." He withdraws his hand. "Let's get you home. Would you like me to carry you?"

I shake my head. That would be too painful. As hard as it is to walk, I'll manage.

Carol huffs and stands. "All right. We'll go home. I still wish you would stay here, though."

The girls gather around, telling me it's okay, that I need to get home and they'll text when they hear more about Maya. All I can do is smile and shuffle my way to the door.

"You need to eat," Carol is saying. "And we can stop and get you—"

"I just need to rest," I say.

She clicks her tongue. "Hannah, stop arguing. I know what I'm talking about."

"She isn't arguing." Michael stands between me and her. "Carol, I know you want to help, but we're going to follow Hannah's lead here, and that's not up for debate."

Tears of gratitude fill my eyes, and I suddenly realize just how badly my aunt's nervousness is wearing me down. What hurts doubly is the fact that she doesn't seem to trust me. She doesn't believe I know how to take care of myself.

With that realization comes another one. The last place I

want to be right now is home. Because that's where Carol is going.

I suck in a painful breath.

"Hannah?" Carol steps around Michael to look at me.

I swallow hard. "I…"

"Come to our house." Katie blinks at me with big, caring eyes. "You can sleep in my room."

It's like she knows exactly what I need when I'm too afraid to admit it to myself. I need peace. Quiet.

Which I can't get with my aunt around, as much as I hate that.

I lick my lips. "That sounds good."

Carol's face is incredulous. "Hannah…"

"I just…need this…" I trail off, exasperated, so tired at this point that my tongue feels like it's made from lead. I'm not even sure how much longer I can speak for.

"I see," she whispers.

"I'll get the truck." Michael jogs through the automatic doors.

Carol looks like she's trying to say something, but she can't get it out. My chest wrings tight. I'm not trying to hurt her, but how can I explain that?

Michael's truck arrives, and Katie and Alexis help me into it, my aunt looking on like a lost puppy.

"I'll text," I tell Carol, voice cracking.

She frowns, eyes glossy, and then I look away.

Guilt fills me as we drive out of the parking lot, but I still know that I'm making the right choice for myself. If I go home with my aunt, she'll hover constantly, and I won't be able to get the rest I need.

Plus, if Michael and Katie are going to be in my life, they'll see me flare eventually, and it's better that they know what it looks like now.

That way, if they don't like what they see, there's still time to get out.

My chest constricts. Maybe this wasn't the right decision. Maybe I should have them both stay here and gone home with my aunt instead. Other than Flick, she's the only person who's ever seen me have a full flare.

Well, them and Paul...

Who told me I was exaggerating the pain, that I was just stressed out.

The memories flood back, and even though I do my best to keep them at bay, they don't go anywhere. I did the right thing and kicked Paul out of my life, but even years later, his cruel words and eagerness to make me wrong still linger.

As does the knowledge that it could all happen again.

So far, Michael has been accepting, but he really doesn't know what he's in for. He has no idea how bad things can get, how limiting it is to have someone like me around.

And once he sees what it's truly like, there's no going back. He'll either accept it... Or he'll leave.

## *Chapter Twenty*

MICHAEL

"What can I get you?" I crouch next to my king-sized bed, where Katie and I have gotten Hannah settled under a pile of blankets.

She smiles at me—which seems to take a lot of effort since she's clearly in pain. "This is good. Thank you."

"We can watch a movie," Katie says.

I'm about to tell her that we need to let Hannah rest—since she wanted to be alone last time, I assume she wants that again—but Hannah speaks up.

"A movie sounds great. What do you want to watch?"

My jaw drops, but I quickly close it and try to hide my flurry of emotions. I'm glad that she decided to come home with us, as I'll be able to keep a close eye on her. Plus, she shouldn't have to leave bed to get herself things. And the whole matter with her aunt is another boatload of issues. What does it say that Hannah didn't feel comfortable enough going home with Carol?

"Anything Disney," Katie says. "I'll go get my DVDs."

She hurries out of the room, and I take advantage of the stolen moment. "You okay?" I ask Hannah.

"Yeah." She smiles from her mountain of pillows. "I'll be better after some rest."

"I mean, when it comes to your aunt." My jaw tightens. The way Carol acted at the hospital was uncalled for. As a parent myself, I get it; she's worried about her niece.

Hannah isn't eleven, though, like Katie. She's a grown woman who's been managing her health on her own for years now. Carol's help was only making the situation more stressful. I could see it in Hannah's pinched face, in how she seemed to grow even weaker every time Carol spoke up.

"I feel bad." She lowers her gaze. "Not going home with her. I just..." Her voice cracks. "She tries to help, but sometimes it's too much, you know?"

"Hey, it's okay." I reach for her hand. "I get it. I know that her intentions are coming from a place of love. I can also see how they can cause more burden than help."

"Yeah." She sighs and looks up at the ceiling. "I've never pushed her away like that."

"You don't need to be sorry."

"I am, though." She twists her lips.

I stroke my thumb across the top of her hand. "It's okay to take breaks from people. I can tell that she just doesn't understand the effect she's having."

"I should tell her." She blinks at the ceiling.

"Another time." I wrap it up at the sound of Katie's approaching footsteps. "Right now, you need to take it easy."

She lifts her head, smiles at me. "Thank you."

"Thank you," I say just as Katie walks into the room. "For trusting me enough to come here."

Her gaze softens, and there's so much more in her expression waiting to come out, but Katie is climbing onto the bed with a stack of DVDs.

"Which one?" Katie spreads the movies out across the bed.

"That one." Hannah points, and Katie gets to work popping in the DVD.

"You should probably eat some dinner." I resist the urge to brush hair off Hannah's forehead, not wanting to hurt her by touching her the wrong way. "How about potato soup? I'll order delivery from the deli."

This time, her smile lights up the room. "That would be delicious. Thank you."

I leave the room to place the order while she and Katie start the movie. It's not until I've arranged the delivery and I'm in the middle of doing the dishes that are in the sink that I realize just how nerve-racking this whole evening has been.

Not only was I concerned about Maya, but setting foot in the hospital was a whole other experience. The last time I was there, it was when my dad died.

And then there's Hannah flaring, which is enough to make me sick with worry. And then, on top of that is Carol's response to Hannah's flare.

But at least everyone is okay now, and there was one bright spot to being in the hospital—seeing Hannah teaching everyone in the waiting room how to knit.

She has a way with people, which she might not even be aware of. While her anxiety comes to the surface during most interactions, she's clearly in her element when teaching. She knows how to make a community, how to bring the light to even the darkest, scariest place—like a hospital waiting room.

And all by being herself.

Or maybe…

I pause, hands in the soapy water.

Maybe that's just how she makes me feel, like the world isn't as heavy as I once thought it was, like there's something wonderful to be found in each and every day.

The doorbell rings with our delivery, my time for reflection over. Drying off my hands, I head to the door.

But it's not our dinner. It's Carol.

She stands tall, her chin tipped up. "Hi, Michael."

"Hey...Carol." I consider inviting her in—that would be the right thing to do, wouldn't it?—but if Hannah hears her voice, she'll become even more stressed. "Hannah is resting."

She nods, but her shoulders tighten even more until they nearly reach her ears. My heart nearly cracks in two, because it's like I see her for the first time. Or, rather, feel her. Feel what she's going through.

"Would you like to have a chat?" I gesture at the chairs on the front porch.

She's stiff as she lowers herself to sit, hands shaking. "This was a bad idea."

"Actually..." I sit in the metal chair next to her, one with peeling paint that I picked up at the secondhand shop. "She's happy over here. She's getting some quiet."

"No. I apologize. I don't mean coming to your house. I mean... Coming to Pine Island. Opening this shop." She sniffs. "It's more than someone in her condition can manage."

"I think Hannah is more resilient than you give her credit for," I say, aware that I'm nearly parroting what Jenny said to me about Katie. "She can handle a lot. She has been handling a lot. Knit Happens is a huge success."

"Yes, but at what expense?" She gives me a sharp look.

I stretch out my legs, considering how best to answer. "If you're anything like me, or most parents, then Hannah is your number one priority. Am I right?"

She doesn't skip a beat. "Of course."

"She told me a little bit... About her mom passing, and her going to live with you. How you taught her how to knit, then came and looked at the storefront for her when she was sick… That's more than most parents would do."

"She needs me." She frowns, worry lines forming between her eyebrows.

"I won't argue that, but is it possible that she doesn't need you as much as you think?"

Carol gazes into my dark yard, and I'd like to think she's considering my words.

"What do you mean?" she finally asks.

"The last time Hannah flared, we were out together. I drove her home. She could barely walk. I wanted to come inside with her." My chest tightens in pain. "So badly. I wanted to take care of her, but she wouldn't let me. I don't know, maybe she didn't want me to see her that way… The point is, she took care of herself. I stayed by my phone for days, ready to run over there if she needed a thing. And she never did. She was good."

Carol twists one of her rings around and around. I take it as my invitation to go on.

"Hannah appreciates everything you've done for her. She has nothing but good things to say about you. And while the fibromyalgia does mean she needs extra care, for the most part, she's able to provide that for herself."

Carol cocks her head at me. "You're trying to tell me she's flown the nest?" She laughs dryly. "And I'm holding her back, clipping her wings?"

I just look at her. It's probably best if I don't answer that.

She seems to do that for herself anyway, because she sighs and looks at her lap. "She's here, at your house, because of me. She doesn't want to be with me."

"She doesn't want to be babied," I correct.

Carol lifts her head and murmurs in agreement. "Here's the thing about kids. You'll see this eventually. They 'grow up' technically, but to their parents, they'll always be little. Someone to be protected at all costs."

"And that's why you're one of the best parents in the world." I mean it one hundred percent.

She dabs at the corners of her eyes. "I need to apologize to her. Not now, of course."

"I'll tell her tomorrow that you came by."

She stands. "I would appreciate that." She takes a step toward the yard then pauses. "You're a good man, Michael. I'm glad Hannah met you."

Emotion clogs my throat—God, I hope she's right, hope I can be the man Hannah needs—so I just nod.

Carol slips into the night, and I watch her car's headlights journey down the road. Standing, I brush the paint off my jeans, remind myself to get some proper chairs once I have the time, and head inside.

I've barely closed the door when I hear another car pull up, though. Our dinner has arrived.

Tipping the driver and grabbing the bags, I dish up the soup and breadsticks and find a serving tray to carry it all on.

Following the sounds of Katie's and Hannah's laughter, I walk across the living room and peek into the bedroom. They're sitting up in bed, watching the newest Disney movie.

An unexpected wave of emotion hits me, so fast and hard that I almost drop the tray.

This is it. What I've been missing out on all these years.

And what Katie has been missing out on as well.

The two of us have been a good team, but something has always been lacking, as much as I didn't want to admit it. I've wanted a woman around, and Katie has needed that as well.

Could this be it? What they call the real deal?

Hannah letting us stay with her this evening suggests that

she's seeing it too. The first time she started flaring around me, she couldn't shut the door in my face fast enough. And now…

She's showing me the most sensitive part of her life. Trusting me with it.

And I get it. I see why she has to plan everything out, why she always has to measure her spoons. I also see why she hides it to some degree—not everyone is understanding.

But I can be. Hell, I can be more than understanding.

I can embrace this part of life. Work with it.

If she'll let me.

Katie notices me hovering outside the doorway. "What are you doing?"

"Uh, nothing. Just didn't want to interrupt what looked like a good part."

I busy myself with distributing the food, and the three of us sit together, eating and watching the movie. I don't register one thing that happens on the screen, though. For me, it's all about who's in this room with me. These two people are the most important ones in the world—it doesn't matter that I've only known Hannah a handful of weeks.

She feels like family. Like the place I've been aching for all these years.

Finished with her soup, Katie snuggles under a throw between Hannah and me, her eyelids getting heavy. Out of the corner of my eye, I see Hannah smiling. Despite her pain and exhaustion, she's happy.

Just as happy as I am right now?

The thought makes my heart so full, it nearly bursts from my chest.

Catching me watching, Hannah looks at me.

*I love you*, I silently mouth.

She gazes at me for a long moment. I don't expect her to say it back. I simply couldn't keep it in any longer, couldn't keep walking around with her not knowing.

*I love you,* she mouths back.

We hold our gaze, and I'm sure that life continues on around us. People go to work. They walk their dogs. Pay their bills. Watch the sunset.

But if that's happening, I wouldn't know it. For me, the whole world is right here, right in front of me.

# Chapter Twenty-One

## HANNAH

"Hold on." Michael jumps out of his truck and hurries around the front of it, but I already have the door open by the time he reaches where I'm at on the passenger's side.

"I can get out," I laugh.

"Okay." He steps back, but his hand is still outstretched. So I take it.

"Only because I want to touch you," I clarify, getting out of his truck and planting my feet in my driveway.

He grins. "I don't care about the reason, as long as you're touching me."

Pushing onto my tiptoes, I kiss him long and good. Love and carnal desire swirl through me, and the kiss deepens. His strong hands find my waist, where they dig into my shirt. He's holding back, probably conscious of the fact that Carol is undoubtedly watching us through the window.

But I don't really care. I'm happy, and I want the whole world to know.

Breaking the kiss, I gaze up into his eyes. "Thank you for driving me home."

"I don't have to leave. I can just hang on you like this. Like a backpack." He demonstrates, draping his arms over my shoulders.

Laughing, I playfully shove him off. "You have to get to work."

"Oh yeah." He grins wickedly. "There's that."

I slide my hand down his arm, feeling the firm muscles popping beneath my fingers. "I'll miss you."

He dips his face and locks gazes with me. "Same," he breathes, like it's the most important word he's ever spoken in his life.

Hard as it is, I step away from him. "I'm going to go in now."

He closes my door and follows me around the truck, his hand on my back, eliciting delicious shivers. "Okay if I watch you walk in?"

Laughing, I shake my head. "Yeah, sure."

I feel his gaze on my back like it's a physical touch, and when I get to the door, I give him a wave. Still smiling, he climbs into his truck, waves goodbye, and drives off.

Magical, romantic moment over. Time to face what's waiting in my house.

Taking a deep breath, I open my front door.

A couple days of rest at Michael's was exactly what I needed, but I still feel a little guilty about leaving my aunt home by herself. Michael told me she stopped by, and we've texted a little since then, but there's been no real conversation.

She looked so crushed in the hospital, like she couldn't possibly comprehend why I would want to be anywhere but with her.

I want to explain my reasoning, and I've spent the last day putting a little speech together, but as I walk into the cottage and find her scrubbing my fridge, I discover I've forgotten English.

"Hi." She straightens up and takes off her rubber gloves. "How are you feeling?"

I swallow, my words slowly coming back to me. "Better. Still a little tired."

"Maya is back home. Did anyone tell you?"

"Yeah. She's doing well, Alexis said." Pulling out a chair, I take a seat at the table. "Thank you for helping out at the shop. Without you and Flick, it just... I would have had to close it."

"Of course." She fills up the teakettle. "Tea?"

"Sure." I lace my hands in my lap. What I need to say feels like a sickness climbing its way up my throat.

Carol sets out two mugs and drops a tea bag into each one. She seems just as uncomfortable as me, except she's trying to beat the feeling back by staying busy.

"About the hospital..." I clear my throat.

"Hannah. I understand." For the first time since I walked through the door, she stops moving.

"I don't want you to think... It's not that I don't want you around."

Carol sits across from me. "I talked to Michael. Well, he talked to me. Made me see some things."

I blink in surprise. "Like what?"

Sighing, she runs her fingers through her loose hair. "I've been treating you like you're still a kid, assuming you need me when you don't."

"I would much rather you do that than not care at all."

She smiles wryly. "There's an in-between, and it's where I've been failing you."

I bite my lip, appreciating her admission but hesitant to agree. It sounds like she's already been hard on herself, and I don't want to kick her when she's down.

"I'm going to back off." She laces her hands on the table. "Not hover so much."

"You don't hover. You're all the way in Oregon—"

"I hover when I'm here." She gives me a hard look. "You're too nice to tell me that, but your boyfriend isn't."

I look down, my face warming in pleasure at hearing Michael be called my boyfriend. "He's pretty up front."

"In the best way. He's a good guy. And Katie is a sweet girl. I'm glad you have them here. Your friends, too."

There's a hint of wistfulness there, and when I look up, her eyes are misty.

"You don't need me like you used to, Hannah Banana," she says, "and that's okay. You know how to handle your health, your life."

Reaching across the table, I take her hand. "I still want you around."

She pats my hand. "I know, and it's even better to be wanted than needed."

I swallow the lump in my throat. "Thank you," I whisper. "For telling me this."

The teakettle whistles, and she gets up to pour the water. "It was all Michael. He made me realize some things."

My heart fills with glitter. I could sing Michael's praises all day long, but that would probably exhaust her.

"Thanks," I say, reaching for the tea she sets in front of me.

"I'm going to head back home tomorrow." She takes her seat and blows on her tea.

"What? No. You don't need to go."

She lifts her hand. "I know, but it will be good for us. I have a list of things to get to back home anyway. I'm thinking of running for HOA president."

"You'd be good at that." I grin.

"Right?" She winks. "I'm so bossy."

"In good ways."

She sips her tea. "You're doing good here, kid. Your mom would be proud."

A complex tornado of emotions crashes through me. I'm feeling everything at once—appreciation, sadness, hope, joy, love—but that's too much to express, so I just settle for a "Thank you."

Over Carol's shoulder, a cardinal comes to the window and pecks at the seed suet hanging there. Another cardinal calls for it, and the first one takes off, wings flapping, suet swinging from the rapid departure.

"This is good tea." I take another sip, and Carol nods and murmurs in response.

# Chapter Twenty-Two

## HANNAH

Hovering my cursor above the "send" button, I hold my breath. This moment feels so big, so special, I'm almost expecting confetti to rain down from the ceiling.

I've done it. I finally finished my funding application. Even with everything going on in my life, even with last week's flare.

A grin spreads across my face, and I click the button. A page pops up telling me that the application has been received, and I smile even bigger.

"I did it," I call out to Flick, who's on the other side of the store, unpacking our latest delivery.

"Of course you did. Now, we just wait for the money to roll in."

"I'm not sure it's like that," I laugh. "But it would be nice."

Flick glances at the clock. "You should probably get going. Didn't you tell Maya you would be there at three?"

"Oh. Yeah! That's right." Sliding off the stool, I stow my laptop in my messenger bag.

"One second. I have something for you." Flick goes to where her jacket is hanging behind the counter and pulls out a small box covered in wrapping paper. "To celebrate finishing the application."

"What?" My jaw drops. "Flick..."

"I know. I know it wasn't necessary, but this is kind of a big deal." She hands me the present. "I'm proud of you."

Tears fill my eyes. Flick gets it; most people wouldn't, but she knows how momentous this achievement is. There are too many reasons not to finish something like a grant application, from chronic pain to hours filled caring for a business. And yet I did it.

She sees that. Just like she always sees me.

Because I don't trust myself to talk right now, I unwrap the box instead. Inside is a silver padding yarn ring.

I gasp with delight. "I love it. Thank you."

"You're welcome." She gives me a big hug. "Tell Maya I say hi."

"I will," I promise, putting the gift into my bag and grabbing my jacket.

"The casserole!"

"That's right." Spinning around, I grab the casserole I made from our mini fridge and dash out the door.

Despite the cold, it's a sunny afternoon. Dried leaves roll down the street as I drive through downtown and into Maya's neighborhood, no fewer than eleven people waving at me along the way. Even though I'm no longer new to the island, it feels like I've crossed into townie territory the last week. People know me. I know them.

And, surprisingly, I don't hate it. Actually, I think I might like it.

At the edge of town, a block from the water's edge, I park alongside the curb next to Maya's house. It's been almost a week since we took her to the hospital, and she's been at home, taking a break from work—and going a little stir-crazy, according to her group texts.

Casserole in hand, I head up the driveway. Next door, Maya's neighbor, Pat, turns off his leaf blower.

"Hey, Hannah. Nice afternoon."

"Sure is." I wave at him—yet another person I feel like I already know so much about, despite hardly knowing each other.

Thanks to Michael, I'm well-informed on how close Pat was with Michael's dad, along with how much Pat disapproves of Michael's firehouse renovations. And that's just small-town life, isn't it? We all know far too much about one another.

It's starting to bother me less, though. If anything, I just shake my head and laugh at it now.

How could I not? The last week, it's like the world has been in Technicolor. The shop has been busy, Carol and I have been talking even more than usual since she went back to Portland, I've felt great after recovering from the flare...and Michael said he loves me.

Butterflies flit through my stomach as I ring Maya's doorbell. Michael loves me!

And I love him.

Is this what true, complete happiness feels like?

Maya opens the door, beaming at me. "Oooh, I'm so happy to see you."

"How are you?" I quickly close the door behind me, worried about her getting too cold.

"Doing better, but I'm ready to go back to work." She leads me into the kitchen.

"I brought you a casserole. Heat it on 350 for about an hour." I slip it into the fridge next to the other casseroles people have dropped off. Man, this town really is supportive. How did I never see it before?

"Thank you. Want some tea?"

We settle onto her couch, where she pours us each a mug from her ceramic pitcher. It's cozy in her little home, piano music playing softly in the background and birds coming to the window feeder.

"I want to say thank you again." She gazes at me over her mug. "For being at the hospital with me. It felt good not to have to go through all of that alone...again. My ex used to go with me to all my appointments, but since we broke up..."

"I get it. It's hard to do that alone."

She smiles ruefully. "It takes some getting used to."

"I'll go to any of your appointments with you. Any time."

"Same." She bites into her smile. "Although, do you really need it? With what's going on with Michael, I don't see him ever missing an appointment."

I press my fingers against my smile. "It feels like a daydream. I never thought I would be in a relationship this amazing."

"You deserve it. You both do."

I sigh happily and glance out the window before turning back to Maya. "I want to live with him and Katie. Is that crazy?"

"No. Not at all."

"I know it's kind of early, but maybe we could move in together this summer. I don't just love him. I love Katie too." My chest warms. "I want to be a family."

"Hannah, that's beautiful—"

My phone rings from inside my purse, cutting her off.

"Sorry." I reach in to see that it's an unknown, but local, number.

"Want to see who that is?" Maya sips her tea.

"Yeah," I mumble, hitting the answer button. "This is Hannah."

"Hannah. Hey. This is Jenny! Michael gave me your number in case I ever needed to call. I hope you don't mind."

"Of course not." I glance at Maya, who can hear the conversation.

"I wanted to let you know that Michael and his crew have been called in to help with a fire on the mainland. It's at the high school, an all-hands-on-deck situation."

My heart flutters. "Okay." Why is she telling me this? Michael has gone out on calls multiple times since we met. Is there something different about today's fire?

"He's safe. I just thought you would want to hear this before people start asking you about it or anything like that."

I want to feel relief over her explanation, but it doesn't come. "Thank you. I do appreciate the heads-up."

"I'll let you know about any updates."

"Okay. Thanks, Jenny."

"Bye." She hangs up.

Even though her call was meant to comfort me, I can't help but feel the opposite. Clearly, she's concerned, or else she wouldn't have reached out to me.

"Is this a big deal?" I ask Maya. "A fire at the high school? Why would she tell me?"

Maya shakes her head. "I don't know," she breathes.

I put my phone down, feeling nauseous and out of my element. Is this what life is like with a firefighter? Random calls about their being in danger?

I stare out the window, my good mood dissipating as a fog of worry comes rolling in.

## *Chapter Twenty-Three*

MICHAEL

Stepping into the high school's main hallway, I take in the two paths. One, leading to the gym and cafeteria, is clear. From the other direction, smoke billows along the lockers.

My team fans out, everyone following their assigned routes to anyone who might be trapped or otherwise in need of assistance. Since it's Sunday and the school was locked when the fire started, there's a good chance no one is in here, but you can never be sure.

I take a step toward the smoke—and then freeze.

It's like weights have been clamped around my ankles. I'm sinking into the floor, unable to move, unwanted images flashing across my mind's eye.

My dad. In a fire similar to this one—on the mainland, on a Sunday. Looking for occupants.

It's when he had his heart attack and collapsed.

My windpipe tightens, but my SCBA is working just fine, pumping air into my mask. It's me that isn't all right.

I haven't been in a fire this big since Seattle, and I thought I could handle it. It's not the fire itself that's challenging me, though. It's what it reminds me of.

My dad.

The man who slipped away in the blink of an eye, before we had a chance to make up.

What if I don't make it out of here alive? Katie will be orphaned. And Hannah...

I shake some sense into myself. I need to keep it together. There could be people in this building relying on my finding them and getting them out safely.

I make my way down the hallway, Red and the rest of my team at my side. "It's all classrooms down this way?" I ask over our comms line.

"Yep," Red, whose kid goes here, confirms.

I nod and push forward, kicking open doors to make sure each room is empty. We round a bend, getting closer to the source of the smoke, when I notice something odd. Flames. At the end of the hallway.

But they're purple.

Shit.

"Where's the chem lab?" I ask Red.

His eyes widen as he gets what I'm suggesting. "At the end of the hallway."

I switch to the main line. "It's a chemical fire! Halt any water use. Get the foams ready."

Why did I not think of this? Of course every high school has a chemistry lab. And with my training in Seattle, I should know better. I was part of a team that handled calls all the time for an industrial park that produced bath and body products.

I haven't had my head screwed on straight; that's my problem. I've been distracted by my own problems since the call came in, too busy feeling sad about my dad.

And now we could all pay for it.

"We need to back out," I bark into the line. "Get chemical protective clothing and move back in."

We hustle out of the building, sweat pouring down my temples, and get into the chemical-resistant suits. Meanwhile, the fire rages behind us, and a crowd of curious onlookers appears. The police drive them away across the lawn, preparing for a possible explosion.

"You okay?" Red eyes my shaking hands as I pull on my gloves.

"Fine. Let's go."

I lead my team back in, with the crew on the outside feeding the hose with foam through a broken window in the chemistry lab. This time, I move with more purpose, determined to get in and out as swiftly as possible.

Lab fires are no joke. It's not a matter of if there will be an explosion—it's when.

My heart hammering at the speed of light, I make my way into the lab, followed by my team. Thank God, the source of the fire is apparent immediately. A glass cabinet has been broken, and in front of it, a beaker of chemicals sits on a lit Bunsen burner.

My lips draw thin. Great. So some teenager pissed at being given detention decided they would blow up the school?

"We need to read the labels first," I tell my team. "To make sure we use the right kind of foam."

I grab one of the containers on the counter and try to read the label, but the smoke makes it nearly impossible.

"Michael?" Red asks. "We need to make a call."

I curse under my breath. "If we use the wrong foam—"

"We don't have time."

He's right. I need to take a shot in the dark, and pray it's the right one.

"Get the AR-AFFF pumping!" I shout across the comms line.

"Copy that," a voice from outside responds.

I put down the container, about to move for the hose, when there's a deafening boom. The whole room shakes, and I'm knocked off my feet.

I hit the ground on my side, the impact sending a shock through my body. Images flash in front of my eyes. Katie playing in our yard with Rose... The fight with my dad—the last time I ever saw him... And Hannah.

Hannah in my house, waking up in my bed every morning. Wearing a wedding dress and saying "I do" as she looks into my eyes. Standing beside me clapping as we watch Katie graduate from high school.

It's the life we could have had, and just as quickly as it's there...it's gone.

I crochet another chain. Then another. Then another.

"Hannah? Would you like anything from Tall Order?"

"Huh?" I look up and blink the person standing in front of me into focus. It's Cynthia. "Oh. I'm fine. Thank you." I put down my crocheting, feeling like an insensitive jerk.

Here I am, sitting in the corner of Knit Happens, worried half to death about Michael. And how must his mother be feeling? I can't even begin to imagine the stress of knowing your child is in a building that just exploded from a chemical fire.

She smiles gently at me. "This is just part of the job, you know?"

A lump forms in my throat. "Yeah," I rasp.

And she'd know. Her husband was also a firefighter—a firefighter who died while fighting a fire.

So how can she so nonchalantly say it's "part of the job"? How can she be so accepting?

I'd never ask her this, and she's gone anyway—out the door to the coffee shop. It's just me...and the other fifteen or so people who have gathered in Knit Happens to wait for news about Pine Island's fire crew.

All that we know is the chem lab at the high school exploded. We don't know if anyone was injured or...worse.

Waiting for this kind of news is the type of hell I wouldn't wish on anyone. Worst-case scenarios keep running through my mind. Michael injured. Michael trapped under rubble. Michael dead.

Swiping at my tired eyes, I catch the news that the group—including several shop owners and Devin, Alexis, and Flick—are watching on a tablet. A shot of smoke drifting skyward fills the screen, with a grim-looking reporter in the foreground. My stomach clenching tight, I look away before I vomit and pick my crochet needles back up.

At least I have this. I can focus on this. I don't have to worry about Michael or Katie, who is with Jenny at home... I can just crochet... One...chain...at...a...

"Hey." Someone touches my shoulder, making me jump.

"Hi," I mumble to Flick, who is crouched in front of me.

"You were falling asleep."

"Was I?" I rub my face. I can't fall asleep. It's barely dinnertime.

"Yeah." Her eyebrows knit together in concern. "How are you doing?"

My brain is slow to formulate an answer. "Fine."

It's a lie. I'm exhausted, that's how I'm doing. I can't think straight, can barely keep my eyes open.

The truth is glaringly obvious—I'm having a fatigue flare.

They're even harder to treat than pain flares. The only thing that helps is lying in a dark room and sleeping for as long as my body needs. But that's impossible right now. I'm too wired.

Not that I need to tell Flick any of this. She's reading it all on my face.

"I can push through," I assure her. "Once I hear about Michael, I'll go home. I promise. But I can't rest until I know that he's okay." She sighs and stands. "I understand."

The front door opens, but I don't bother looking to see who it is. Instead, I drop my head against the wall and close my eyes. Just a few minutes of rest, then I'll open them back up.

"...flare," Flick says to someone, her voice sounding like it's on the other side of the room.

"...do for it?" Someone—Cynthia?—asks.

A phone rings. Like every other sound, it's distant, foreign. There's a moment of talk and then an exclamation of joy.

"Everyone is safe!" Pat calls out.

My eyes pop open, and I sit up straight. "Michael's safe?" I croak.

Flick hugs me. "He is. They all are."

I touch my cheeks and find that they're wet. How long have I been crying?

"I'm going to take you home." Flick gently urges me up. "Then come back and lock up."

"I'll take her." Cynthia steps forward, looping her arm through mine.

I want to protest—being taken home and put to bed never stops being embarrassing—but I don't have the strength for that. Instead, I let Cynthia load me into her car.

"I'm sorry," I murmur, curled up in her passenger's seat like a child.

Cynthia clucks. "Oh no, don't say that. You don't have to apologize to me."

"I'm glad Michael is okay," I murmur, doing my best to keep my eyes open.

She pats my shoulder. "Me too."

Giving her directions to my cottage proves about as challenging as solving a Rubik's Cube, and by the time we pull into my driveway, I'm more zombie than human. She walks me inside and helps me into bed.

"What can I do for you?" she asks.

"Nothing, thank you." I snuggle deeper under the covers. "I just..." I yawn. "...need to sleep."

"Of course." She shuts off the light and tiptoes out of the room.

"Cynthia?"

"Yes?"

"Say hello to Katie?" I ask.

"Certainly. Sleep tight."

The boards in the house creak as she walks across the living room and lets herself out the front door. Her headlights cut through my bedroom window, and I stare at the glass even after they're gone.

It's the second time in a week that I've been tucked into bed by a member of Michael's family, and the guilt is heavy. This isn't what any of them signed up for. One time is fine, but taking care of someone like me on a regular basis can quickly become exhausting.

Remembering that gives me more sympathy for my aunt. Her ability to hover now looks more like a superpower than an annoyance.

Have I made a mistake getting involved with Michael? Is our relationship proving to do more harm than good to him and his family?

And what about me? My worry today about Michael has caused a flare.

What happens when he's in another fire? It's not like I can turn off the part of me that's concerned about him. Undoubtedly, I'll flare again since emotional distress is a big trigger. And that will suck for both me and him—and his family.

Tears fill my eyes. I've changed so much of my life to make it fibromyalgia-friendly, but the cold, hard truth is that there are a lot of things that don't fit into this lifestyle. Like teaching full time. Playing sports. Having more than one cocktail per weekend.

Or having a boyfriend who is a fire chief.

As long as Michael and I are together, I'll worry about him. And I don't think I can handle the emotional toil of loving someone who has such a dangerous job. Sure, I'll have the comfort of our relationship, but I'll also have the fear of losing him at any moment. I'll be doing serious damage to my mental and physical health.

Is it really fair to put myself through that? To put Michael through that?

Tears slide down my face as I stare at the dark window, waiting for answers that never come.

## *Chapter Twenty-Five*

MICHAEL

hecking my phone for probably the hundredth time this morning, I frown. Still no text from Hannah.

Is she not feeling well? Or just busy at the shop?

Hoping it's the latter, I slide the phone into my pocket and leave the firehouse. The walk to Knit Happens is lined with scarecrows, inflatable ghosts, and pumpkins—a reminder that Halloween is on its way.

A smile pulls at my lips. Usually, I leave the dressing up to Katie, but I'd be down with a costume this year. Especially if Hannah would like to do some sort of cheesy couples costumes, where we match or play off each other.

I used to shake my head at that kind of thing, but now I look forward to it. More so after yesterday.

When I blacked out in the high school, I thought it was all over. That I'd never see my daughter or Hannah again. And there's nothing that makes you get your priorities straight like staring death in the face.

I don't want to waste any more time. I've told Hannah I love her, but that's not enough. I'm tired of trying to make our

175

crazy schedules sync so we can slip in an hour or two together, tired of coming home and not seeing her face.

It's time to ask her to move in with me.

The thought fills my chest with butterflies, and I pick up the pace, crossing the street and opening the door to Knit Happens.

It's not Hannah at the counter, though. It's Flick.

I stop just inside the entrance, the door falling closed behind me. "Good morning. Is Hannah here?"

"Um." Flick looks up from the yarn catalogue she's flipping through. "She's at home. Having a flare."

I blink. She is? Why didn't she tell me?

Maybe this is a really bad one. She did respond to my text yesterday telling her I was fine after the fire, but after I followed up by saying I needed to see her, she went dark. Has she been curled up in bed this whole time, too in pain to even pick up her phone?

"Shit." I rub my jaw. "Okay. I'll go see her. Do you know if she needs anything brought over?"

"Uh...Michael?" She reaches out a hand. Stops. Purses her lips and looks away.

"What?" I cock my head. There's something she isn't telling me. "What is it?"

Her throat rolls with a swallow. "It's more than just the flare," she whispers. "Yesterday was really hard on Hannah. Seeing you in danger, not knowing if you'd be all right... It took a toll on her."

I feel my eyebrows rise. "It wasn't exactly a walk in the park for me either."

And not just because my team and I were in danger. Being in that fire brought up so much about my dad—regrets that I didn't know I still had.

He was right about Katie, as much as I haven't wanted to

admit it. Hell, he was right about the firehouse kitchen too. I've been stumped when it comes to the renovations, but his plans show that he knew exactly what to do.

Most of all, he was right when it comes to family and community. Right about how important it is to keep our bonds strong, to spend every day we have with the people we love, because we never know which breath will be our last.

Flick sighs. "I know, and I'm not trying to diminish your experience. I'm sorry about that."

I push my fingers through my hair, frustrated. "I'm sorry too. I didn't mean to snap. Her flare... What caused it?"

She smiles, but it's a sad one. "Emotional stress is a big trigger."

My mouth goes dry. Got it. Emotional stress, like the kind you experience when someone you love is in danger.

Is it my fault Hannah flared?

That's a hard pill to swallow, but I already know I'm being too hard on myself, and it's no one's fault. It's not her fault that she has fibromyalgia, and it's not my fault some wannabe pyro lit that Bunsen burner. This is just life. We're dealt certain cards, and we play them to the best of our ability.

The only thing I know for sure is that, no matter what cards we hold, I want to be seated next to her at the table. Always.

"I need to see her." Before Flick can answer, I'm out the door and jogging for where my truck is parked at the firehouse.

Ten minutes later, I knock on Hannah's door, palms sweaty and heart racing. I need her in my arms so bad that I have the shakes. I need to kiss her, tell her I love her, that she means the world to me. If I can do that, everything will melt away.

The stress from the fire. The fear that I put her through. It'll all be gone.

The door opens, and she stands there, dressed in an over-sized sweater and leggings, bags under her eyes.

"Hey," I breathe.

"Hi."

Gently, in case she's in pain, I pull her into my arms. When she wraps her arms around me, I tighten the hold.

"I love you," I breathe into her hair, tears pricking my eyes. "God, Hannah, I'm so happy to see you. Last night, all I could think about was you. How are you feeling? Flick said you're having a flare."

Drawing back, I study her face, heavy with fatigue. "I can stay here with you unless I get a call to go in. Have you eaten today?"

Her eyebrows knit together. "You have a bruise." She touches the welt on my temple.

I shrug. "It's no big deal. I've had worse."

She drops her hand and backs away like she's been shocked.

"What's wrong?" I suddenly feel cold all over.

"Thank you for coming to check on me." She wraps her arms around herself. "The best thing you can do, though, is give me space."

I can't help it. I laugh. "Space? Why?"

She licks her lips, avoiding my eyes. "I need time to think. What happened yesterday...it made me realize that maybe we're going too fast. You know, jumping into a relationship before either one of us is ready."

"I'm ready." My chest swells, full of desire and frustration that need to be released. "Hannah, I want to be with you. Every day. Always. I know last night was scary. That was your first time seeing me on a call like that, and it makes sense that you were spooked. What we need right now, though, is more time together. To work through our feelings around last night and talk about next steps. Hannah, I...I want you to move in with us."

Her gaze flicks to mine, and I see something bright there—

excitement?—before the wall comes back up. "I need time to think, Michael. A...few days."

It's like I've swallowed a whole pile of rocks, and they line my stomach and throat. "Is this about your flare? Are you worried that I'll trigger more of them?"

She sighs. "That's not the issue. Of course I hate having flares, but they don't shorten my life or anything. It's about..." Her voice cracks. "Losing you. If you died in one of these fires, it would break my heart, and it— I can't take any more heartbreak. I don't think I can go through losing someone I love again." She presses her sweater sleeve to her wet eyes. "So, I need some time to decide whether I can...cope with that risk."

Her gaze holds mine for a moment before breaking away. I reach for her, but she steps back, and all the hope and excitement I built up for us crumbles to the ground. I'm a husk of the man I was driving over here, no more than one of the scarecrows set out for Halloween.

"Hannah," I rasp, but what can I say to that? She has the right to make her own choices, just like everyone else. "Okay," I finish, lamely, stupidly, disappointed in myself for not correcting this course we were on before it was too late.

"See you later," she whispers.

She shuts the door, and I stand on her porch like the sorry son of a bitch I am. A reject. Someone who has tried his hardest but still isn't good enough. I could put out every fire on the East Coast, dazzle and astonish Hannah in every way, give her anything and everything a man could ever provide a woman—a beautiful home, children, affection—but I can't take away the uncertainty that comes with life.

And so I trudge back to my truck without a clue where to go from here.

# *Chapter Twenty-Six*

## HANNAH

"How many students are there again?" I ask, embarrassed to have forgotten.

But Maya isn't fazed at all. "Fourteen."

"Right." I nod and finish arranging the chairs in her classroom. It's the first crafting class at the elementary school since I turned Michael away from my door, and to say I'm nervous is an understatement.

Does Katie know about what happened between her dad and me? Even if he didn't tell her anything, she's such a perceptive kid that she probably knew something was off the moment he walked through the door. Plus, I've been over my flare for a few days, and I haven't been around. That alone speaks volumes.

My stomach in knots, I pull out the kids' projects, which Maya keeps in baskets on the shelves. Even though my energy is back, I feel worse than I have in years. All I can think about is Michael's crushed face when I told him I needed space.

And right after he said he wanted to move in together, which is the real kicker.

I could have told him that I want the same thing, that

waking up next to him every morning and driving Katie to school would be a dream come true. But that would be salt in both our wounds.

It was such a huge step for him to even mention moving in together, and I'm afraid that I ruined things between us by asking for space. Maybe I should have kept my mouth shut and been more optimistic.

But I know I couldn't have done that. The fear wouldn't dissipate; it would just be stuffed down to come up another day. I know my limits, and it's only smart to question whether I can handle another serious relationship. Especially one with a person whose job carries so much risk.

And yet, I'm aching to talk to him. It feels like a chemical withdrawal, like one little text from him could bring me back from the edge.

The universe must hear my prayers, because my phone beeps. Desperate to see if it's Michael, I claw at my jeans pocket.

It's an email, though—which makes my heart sink. Except... Wait...

I click on the notification, my pulse picking up. Could this be...?

I quickly scan the email.

"What?" Maya asks.

"My grant application was accepted." I look up from the screen. "I'm getting the funding for the store. I can hire another employee now."

"That's great!"

Yeah. It is.

So why don't I feel happier?

I open my texts, about to tell Michael the good news, then stop. What am I doing? I told him I needed a few days to think. It's not appropriate in any way for me to text him updates about my life.

"I'll take you out for a drink tonight to celebrate," Maya is saying as she finishes setting up the classroom.

I nod and put on a smile, but inside, I feel hollow. I spent months working toward this success, but it doesn't feel the same without Michael to share it with.

By not having him in my life, I'm avoiding some potential pain...but I'm also missing out on some joy too. So then, is being without him really worth it?

There's no time to think about it, because the kids are spilling into the classroom. I hastily put my phone away and get started teaching the knitters a moss stitch and the crocheters a shell stitch. The whole while, I can feel Katie's eyes on me. Aside from a smile and a quick "Hey," though, I keep my teacher hat on and focus on the lesson.

"If anyone needs help, I'll be right here." I settle on one of the cushions near the front of the room, Maya sitting at her desk creating a lesson plan.

To no surprise, Katie approaches. "I made you this." She hands me a wonkily knitted thing that looks like some kind of sleeve.

"Oh. Thank you." I take it, my heart filling with warmth. It doesn't even matter that I have no clue what it is. The fact that she made me something makes me want to cry—and because of the whole soup of emotions that comes with this complicated situation.

"It's a case for your glasses," she explains.

I gasp with true delight. "Katie, I love it."

Katie folds her arms and fidgets, looking uncharacteristically uncomfortable. "I want you to know that no matter what happens between you and my dad, we can still be friends."

I hold the crocheted case close to my chest. She's tugging on heartstrings I didn't even know I had. "I'd like that," I say softly.

"Do you have any idea of what I could make for him to cheer him up? He's been down since the fire."

"He has?" A lump forms in my throat.

Katie nods and searches my face, maybe looking for an answer as to what happened between Michael and me?

It doesn't seem like my place to tell her the story, though. It's up to Michael to decide how much or how little she's privy to.

"I'll think about what that could be," I say.

Instead, I spend the rest of the class toggling between feeling sure I've made a terrible mistake by stepping back from Michael and knowing for sure that a life without him is what's best for me. By the time the bell rings, Katie and I can only say a quick goodbye before she leaves with her class, so I'm spared from admitting I haven't come up with any ideas.

"I'll text you," I tell Maya, blowing her a kiss as I grab my bag and walk out of the classroom. School is over, the halls over-flowing with kids.

I keep my eyes peeled, my breath in my throat, hoping to see Michael here picking up Katie and Rose. What would I even say to him, though?

*I'm sorry? I hate this?*

Both are true, but saying them won't do any good. My feelings don't change reality. No matter how much I miss him, I'm probably still better off flying solo.

"Hannah," a woman's voice calls as I'm walking through the front doors.

I spin on my heel and catch sight of Cynthia over the sea of children's heads. My heart jumps into my throat.

*Oh no.* Michael's mom.

Did he tell her about our talk? What does she think about me now?

As she advances toward me, a smile on, I realize I have

nothing to worry about. If anyone understands how I feel, it's Cynthia. Her husband was a firefighter, after all—and he died while at work.

She reaches me, a little breathless from trying to catch up. "How are you? I heard that you and Michael...well..." She smiles, like she's unsure how to finish and that's the best she can do.

For some reason, that breaks my heart more than anything else this last week.

"I'm okay," I say, voice cracking and tears filling my eyes. "How are you?"

"Oh, honey." Her faces scrunches with sympathy. "Would you like to get a cup of coffee? There's a spot a few blocks away. The girls have their play rehearsal today, and I'm hanging around until they're finished."

Because I don't trust myself to speak, I just nod. Cynthia leads us across the parking lot and down the street. With the cacophony of school behind us, she finally speaks.

"So, you and Michael broke up."

Is that what this was? A breakup?

I guess so. I just haven't wanted to call it that. Instead, I've been using gentler phrases, like "taking space" and "figuring things out." There's no guarantee we'll get back together, though. Three days later and I haven't found any additional clarity.

"Yeah." The word is dry as sawdust. It sticks to my mouth and sits there, turning sour till I think I might throw up. "It's for the best, though. I miss him, but I wouldn't have been able to handle worrying about him every time he left the house for work."

Cynthia hums in acknowledgment. "I understand the feeling. Half the time Michael's dad left to go to the firehouse, I felt so nervous."

A little bit of tension leaves my body. It feels good to be seen, even if that in itself doesn't fix any problems.

We reach the coffee shop, which isn't nearly as cute as the one on Pine Island but—according to Cynthia—has good teas. After grabbing two cups of herbal to go, we find seats at one of the wooden tables.

"I'm glad that you understand." I fiddle with my tea bag.

"Oh, I do." She blows on her tea. "But you know, for me, our life together was worth every ounce of the worry."

I freeze, surprised. "It was?"

"Ted loved his job." Her eyes sparkle at a memory that only she's privy to. "Every day, he walked out of the house to a career that he loved, to a job that helped people. It's why he started firefighting in the first place. He wanted to give back to the island that had done so much for his family."

I stare into my tea, mixed emotions rising to the surface. When she puts it that way, I feel like a selfish jerk for not accepting Michael's important job. Then again, I can't give back to the world myself if I'm always having flares, always worried about where he is and if he's okay.

Cynthia goes on. "I suspect that's why Michael took the chief job when it came up."

I look up. "To help people?"

"To give back to the community that raised him."

I have to sit on that one for a minute. Michael always seems so put off by the islanders, annoyed that everyone's nose is in his business.

"I know he doesn't show it," Cynthia says, "but Michael loves Pine Island, even if it isn't the easiest place to live. And Michael..." She lets out a little sigh. "Well, doing anything that didn't help its people wouldn't fill his cup enough. You know what I mean?"

I nod slowly. "I do."

# CHAPTER TWENTY-SIX

"I heard you used to be a teacher."

"Yeah," I say, disappointed that the conversation is straying away from Michael. "I taught at a high school, then when my fibromyalgia started getting bad, I switched to online."

"And then you opened Knit Happens."

"I put everything into it." I laugh at the memory, a rare event where I took a chance. "I had never even been to Pine Island, had never run my own business…"

"But your heart called you to it."

"Exactly."

"So then, you understand." She peers at me over her glasses. "Running that shop makes you happy in a way that teaching didn't, so you switched, even though being a small business owner isn't nearly as safe or steady as teaching."

"No." I blow out a breath. "It isn't."

"But was it worth the risk?"

"One hundred percent," I say with zero hesitation.

Her phone beeps, and she checks it. "Oh! School needs me back. The drama teacher has to go pick up her sick kid from day care. Looks like I'm filling in as director for the day."

"Good luck." I smile. "Thanks for the tea, and for…being here."

She grabs her purse and stands. "You don't have to, but maybe think about what I said."

She steps out into the autumn afternoon, a gust of cool air taking her place. I stay in my seat, staring out the window, her words swirling around in my head.

For years, I've been calculating risks. Counting spoons. Measuring my energy. It's the only way I've been able to get this far in the world while living with a chronic disease.

But is it possible that I've been *too* careful? In my attempts to participate in daily life, is it possible that I've been missing out on opportunities to truly live?

# Chapter Twenty-Seven

## MICHAEL

I stare at the papers on my desk, numbers blurring into one another. Sitting up straight, I rub my eyes and try to blink away the exhaustion.

Maybe tonight, I'll finally be able to sleep, but I doubt it. Since Hannah pretty much kicked me off her porch a week ago, I haven't been able to rest more than thirty minutes. That moment keeps playing over again and again in my head, with me always trying to figure out how I could have done things differently.

But this isn't a fire. There's no perfect protocol. No science that will extinguish the flames and get everyone out alive. Being in my life or not is Hannah's choice.

And what I want doesn't matter.

Picking up my phone, I find my notifications still at zero. Those few days she needed to think have turned into seven, still with no word from her.

A knock on the open office door makes me look up. My mom stands in the firehouse hallway, a plate covered with aluminum foil in her hand.

"I brought you dinner," she says. "Since Katie's at that sleepover tonight, I figured you might not even think about eating."

Despite how annoying her random pop-ins are, I have to laugh. She knows me well.

"Guilty as charged." I put down my phone, and she sets the plate on the table. Her homemade chicken and dumplings—my favorite.

I cock an eyebrow at her. Something is up.

We've barely spoken since that argument in my kitchen, with all of our interactions being limited to info about Katie. And my mom isn't too big to say sorry, but she's also frugal with her apologies.

"How are you doing?" She takes the chair in front of my desk.

"Good." I nod...then keep nodding, unsure of what else to add.

She knows about my breakup with Hannah—hell, who doesn't?—but I'm not about to spill my guts to her just because she asked.

She fiddles with her bracelets. "I want to apologize. I shouldn't have called you hardheaded or second-guessed your ideas for the station. I sometimes forget that you and your dad really are different people. I know how awful that sounds. It's just... I see so much of him in you. And, I suppose, seeing the station done up the way Dad wanted it would have given me the last...*new* memory of him."

I slump back in my chair, feeling like a complete asshole. Of course the kitchen renovation is one of the last connections she has to my dad. Why wouldn't it be that way?

And how come I didn't see this before?

I already know the answer. I was too busy being butthurt to empathize with her.

"I'm sorry, Mom," I sigh. "That makes sense. We can go back to his plans—"

"No." She gives me a hard look. "The station is yours now. You're doing a great job as fire chief, and you need to do what you think is best. This renovation should never have been about my trying to connect with your father. It's your time to shine... and it's my time to trust you."

I'm so taken aback that I don't even know what to say. It's everything I needed to hear but didn't know I needed to. I never realized how important her support is to me.

"Thank you," I settle for mumbling. "I appreciate that. There's...more to it for me. It hit hard when you asked me to do what Dad wanted because..."

My chest constricts. Can I even go through with admitting this?

But she sits there patiently, waiting, and we've come so far in this conversation already. Why not go all the way? Clear every inch of air between us?

"It's complicated," I say, "the way I feel about Dad. When we last spoke..."

"It was an argument."

"Right." I grimace. "Exactly. What he said about me not raising Katie right, it still haunts me. Even though I brought her back here. And it makes me question everything else I do too. Then whenever you or anyone on this island second-guesses me —" I shake my head, still holding on to some pride and not willing to admit how insecure all this shit makes me feel.

"I shouldn't have done that," she says. "And as far as your father goes, he did struggle with you always doing things your own way. That's no secret. He loved Pine Island and couldn't understand why you wanted to move off it. He always assumed that you would come back when you had a family, and your not doing that was even more perplexing. But those were his limitations to deal with, and it was unfair of him to take his emotions out on you. He knew that...even if he never said it."

I catch her eye. "He did?"

She nods once. "Yes. He regretted what he said that night, Michael. I know he did, even if he never apologized."

I sigh, wondering if I can believe her, the person who knew my father better than anyone. Then again, why not let myself believe her? Why not give myself the gift of releasing this burden?

"You're a wonderful father to Katie," she says. "You always have been, whether in Seattle or on the island. Deep down, your father knew that."

I nod, my throat too thick to speak. It feels like a weight has been lifted from my shoulders. The heartbreak from what happened with Hannah is still here, but at least I feel a little lighter—like I can go forth in the world trusting everything will be all right.

It's not like I'll never second-guess my parenting or my job as chief again, but I feel more confident knowing that my parents never thought I was a complete screwup.

"Have you heard from Hannah?" she asks.

The change in topic takes me by surprise, and I gape at her. "Uh...no. And I'm not expecting to."

"Oh." She stands and buttons her coat. "Well, don't give up just yet. She might need some more time to come around to her true feelings, is all."

I digest that, wanting to ask more, but she's already out the door. I'm left alone in the office, my dinner in front of me, new questions swirling in my head.

Does my mom know something I don't? Does it even matter?

Fixating on Hannah will get me nowhere. The best thing I

can do is focus on my life—my kid, my work, bettering myself—and stay open to the possibility that somehow, someday, Hannah and I will find our way back to each other.

# Chapter Twenty-Eight

## HANNAH

"Have you talked to Michael at all?" Maya whispers, sidling up next to me.

I glance at her art class, busy knitting and crocheting away. It's been a week since Katie asked me to help her create a present to cheer up her dad, and I still don't have an answer for her.

I don't have an answer when it comes to anything.

"No," I admit to Maya.

I want to talk to Michael. Of course I do. Just like I want to be with him, just like I want his arms around me every night and his smile greeting me every morning.

But I feel frozen by the unknown. Things might be simple in my little bubble that encompasses Knit Happens and my weekly classes and meetups with the girls—and a flare here and there—but at least I know what to expect. The biggest curve balls that come my way are having to shut down the shop for a day because of a flare or scrambling to find supplies when an order is late coming in.

I'm safe here in this bubble. Lonely, yes. But safe.

The bell rings, and the kids abandon their projects—all

except Katie and Rose, who keep their heads diligently bent over their work.

"Okay, everyone," Maya calls. "Gather your things."

Katie looks up and right at me, questions in her eyes. Questions I'm not sure I have answers to.

Standing, she strides over to me. "Have you come up with anything for my dad yet?"

I draw a deep breath. "Uh...no. But you know him a lot better than I do, so whatever you decide to make for him, I know he'll love."

Her face falls in disappointment. "Oh."

I feel like I've kicked a puppy. Is this part of some plan she has to get Michael and me back together?

My heart wrenches. "I can help you brainstorm."

Her lips twist. "He likes this cartoon. *Gravity Falls.*"

My heart breaks as I remember the date in the fishing shed when we watched that. "Oh. Okay. You could do some amigurumi and crochet him a character from the show."

She nods slowly. "Yeah. I think Dad would like that."

"What would I like?" Michael's voice asks, and I freeze.

My gaze darts to the door, where the last few kids are filing out. Only Maya and Rose are still in the classroom. And Michael.

Tall, strong, dependable Michael. A lighthouse in the darkest night. The man who has gone above and beyond for me multiple times.

Not once has he turned his back on me because of fibromyalgia. Not once has he gotten angry because plans have changed. Never has he treated me like some kind of invalid. And if it's ever frustrated him, he's never shown it.

So what am I doing, pushing him away? Don't I know that it doesn't get better than what's standing right here in front of me?

I could live the rest of my life in a bubble of semi-predictability, but the joy I feel will never come close to what I've experienced with Michael. Being with him, taking a chance with him, is the best choice for me.

No—it's the only choice.

I swallow hard, my heart racing a million miles an hour. "Katie has been trying to think of something to make you to cheer you up...since you've been down lately."

He blinks, mouth dropping open in surprise. He quickly collects himself, though, as I bite my lip. Should I have not said that? I don't have a game plan here, other than, hopefully, ending up back with Michael.

"Yeah." He clears his throat. "I haven't been feeling that great."

His gaze darts over my shoulder, and I turn to see Maya, Rose, and Katie all watching us. My face warms.

Maya tries to play it off by walking past us and fiddling with some artwork on the wall, but the two girls just blatantly stare at us. Katie even raises her eyebrows, urging us to go on.

"Um." I shove my hands into my jeans pockets. "Yeah, I haven't been feeling great either."

"You're over your flare, it looks like. That's good." His gaze softens as he drinks me in, real concern there, and I realize how worried he must have been about me this last week and a half. "Would you like to talk in the hallway?"

"Yes," I nearly shout.

I follow him into the hallway, empty except for the occasional footsteps and voices echoing along the walls. Taking my hands from my pockets, I fold my arms. Then twist my fingers. Then smooth my hair.

I don't know what to do, don't know how to start this conversation.

So, maybe I should just go for it. Take the leap from the

plane and embrace the free fall, no matter what the outcome is —be it soaring like a bird or hitting the ground with a splat.

"I'm sorry," I say, and the words just flow forth, like the cork has been popped and I can't stop them even if I want to. "I made a mistake. I want to be with you, Michael. I love you and Katie, and yes, I want to move in with you. The idea of losing you, yeah, it scares me, but breaking up just because of that fear would be punishing myself. It doesn't make any sense. There's always risk to life, and I—I love what you do."

Tears fill my eyes, and I let them fall. "You help people. You're a true hero, and I'm so proud of you. You're...you're amazing."

I draw a deep breath and wait. Michael just stares at me, studying every inch of my face. It's impossible to read his thoughts, and inside, I have my fingers crossed, praying that he forgives me and takes me back.

And if he doesn't...

I'll live, but will I ever get over it?

No. Because a man like Michael Greer only comes along once in a lifetime, and I would be stupid to think I'd ever meet someone half as amazing as him again.

"Hannah." He steps closer, so close I have to tilt my head back to look at him. His hands find mine, fingers twisting together, and it's like I'm drawing the first breath of my life. Like I didn't know I was only half alive until now, this moment when he smiles down at me, blessing me with his love.

"I love you," he says simply, reaching up to touch my cheek. "And after I kiss the hell out of you, I'm renting a moving truck and taking your things to my place. Tomorrow."

I half laugh, half sob, and his lips crash into mine, stealing my breath and my heart. He slips his arms around my waist, cradling me close. Everything in the whole universe slides into perfect synchronicity, and it just clicks.

# CHAPTER TWENTY-EIGHT

Me. Him. Together.

What could be more right?

The classroom door opens behind us, and I break the kiss to look over my shoulder.

Katie and Rose poke their heads out the door. "Are you back together yet?" Katie asks. "Because I just found a unicorn pattern I want to do instead of Dad's gift."

Michael and I both burst into laughter.

"You can get started on that." Michael's hands linger at my lower back, and I can feel how much he's restraining himself in front of the kids. "We're back together."

Katie's eyes widen. "Yes!"

She and Rose slip back into the classroom, and Michael pulls me close again, pressing his lips to mine and filling the whole world with glitter—and unicorns.

Lots and lots of unicorns.

## Chapter Twenty-Nine

MICHAEL

Standing back, I study the appetizers spread across the firehouse kitchen. Potato skins. Pigs in blankets. Cheese and crackers. Olives.

It's nothing too fancy, but for someone who has never hosted a fundraiser before, I feel I've done a pretty good job. It's not like people will be here for the snacks anyway. Tonight's fundraiser is Pine Island's event of the week, so people will show up just to socialize and get an inside look at the firehouse.

"That looks good," a light, musical voice says behind me.

Grinning big, I spin around and pull Hannah into my arms. She nearly drops her basket of scarves, hats, and gloves, but I grab it in time and set it on the table. "You look good."

She rolls her eyes but smiles. "Really. I didn't know you were so skilled at hosting parties."

"All I did was make some appetizers," I chuckle. "As far as hosting goes..."

"It'll be fun." She throws one of the scarves around my neck and uses it to draw me closer.

"Yeah." I kiss the corner of her lips. "It will be," I murmur, although all I'm really thinking about is getting her alone later.

With Katie sleeping over at Rose's, we'll have the house to ourselves.

I start to kiss her again, but Pat comes into the kitchen, interrupting the moment. "Hey, Michael. I took a look at the new blueprint. It'll work just fine, though I'm not sure about the colors of some of these fittings."

Hannah gives me a wink before stepping away. "I'll go put these pieces with the other donations." She grabs her basket and walks her fine ass out of the room.

"Uh, you were saying...the faucet?" I turn to Pat, my mind completely scrambled, like it always is when my girlfriend is around.

"The fittings." He helps himself to a potato skin.

"Oh, right. Well, I'm sure it will all work out." I lean against the counter, not worried one bit.

I already changed the blueprint a bit to appease Pat, and if he wants to order different fittings, I won't fight him on it. Either way, the new kitchen will have everything it needs.

I'm also not worried about tonight's fundraiser. It's mostly a formality; we'll probably have all the money we need for the renovation within twenty minutes. The whole island is invested in this station, eager to support it.

Eager to support *me*.

It took me a little while to really see that. And yeah, sometimes I still chafe when people in town compare me to my dad, but I know they're doing it because they miss him.

Just like I do.

"I'll come by in the morning," Pat says. "Help you total up the cost of the renovation and see what we can do with the raised money."

"Thanks, Pat. I appreciate it." I follow him out of the kitchen and to the living area, which is full of chairs and a microphone at the front of the room.

The area is already stuffed way past fire code, but for once, I choose to overlook that. Having this many people show up—at least fifty of them, and with more entering as I look—makes me warm all over.

Finding Hannah, I slip my arm around her waist. "Hey."

"Hey." She nuzzles my neck. "Did you—"

"Hannah!" Katie runs over, her newly finished unicorn scarf hanging from her neck, and grabs Hannah's hand. "Carol is helping Rose and me decorate the Christmas tree! Come on! We have new ornaments."

Hannah gives me an apologetic look, but I just blow her a kiss. We'll have plenty of time together later, and Katie's love for Hannah is the biggest blessing in my life. Without their happiness, nothing means anything.

Hannah follows Katie through the crowd and to the Christmas tree in the corner, where her aunt and Rose are wrapping garlands around its branches, and Red comes up to slap me on the shoulder.

"You ready to take the mic and lead this thing?" he asks.

I look at the assembled crowd, all the people watching me expectantly, all the people here to support their fire station and the legacy that my dad left.

All the people who care. All the people who have my back through thick and thin. My community. My home.

"Yeah," I tell Red. "I'm ready."

* * *

"Did you see what Flick won?" I ask Hannah as I park the truck in front of the house.

"The basket from the vet's office?" She smiles. "Yeah. She looked so shocked." A thoughtful look comes across her face.

"Do you think my aunt is really happy staying at the bed-and-breakfast and not with us?"

"I saw her out there pulling weeds this morning." I snort. "If she has something to do, I'm sure she's happy. They're probably thrilled to have the free help too."

"True." She giggles.

I quickly unbuckle my seat belt and rush around the truck to open her door, disappointed that she beats me to it.

"Sorry," she says. "I'm eager to get inside."

"It is cold." I take her hand in mine, hoping that it's not too chilly out here for her.

"No, that's not why." She unlocks the house and pulls me closer.

Getting the hint, I kick the door shut behind us. My hands dance across her body, eager to do the impossible and touch every inch of her all at once. We kick off our boots, drop our jackets.

"Too many clothes," I murmur against her lips as we scramble to remove yet another layer.

Hannah laughs and tugs on my pants. Tired of not already being in the bedroom, I scoop her up and carry her down the hallway. In our room—I never get tired of calling it that—I set her on the bed and quickly remove the rest of our clothes.

She's soft and warm. Tender and secure. Everything I want in a woman and more. My dream come true.

Climbing on top of her, I link our hands together. Fingers pressed into the mattress, I drag my lips down her neck and shoulder. She arches her back, pushing her hips against my thighs.

Seizing her ass, I give it a light squeeze. Fire scars through my groin. I'm hard and aching to be buried inside her, and luckily, she's giving me all the signs that she wants the same. Gently,

I push into her, her eyes closing and her mouth dropping open in pleasure.

She's already eager for more, though. Grabbing my hips, she pushes her pelvis into mine.

"Greedy tonight," I chuckle.

She grins at me, her eyes hooded. "You have a problem with that?" she rasps.

"Not at all," I growl, before driving deeper into her.

We wind together, wild and unchecked. She wraps her legs around mine, urging me on. We're a tornado of kisses, of desperate grunts and moans. I can feel her tightening around me, getting closer to release.

She explodes, fingernails digging into my back, and I let go as well, releasing deep inside her. We're perfectly united, our souls, hearts, and bodies one.

Collapsing onto the mattress, I pull her onto my chest and kiss her lips. "I need to thank Jenny."

"What?" Hannah shrieks, lifting her head to look at me. "Explain to me why, after we just had sex, you're talking about thanking your sister?"

I roll my eyes and laugh. "If it weren't for her setting us up, we wouldn't be here tonight. She deserves a really good Christmas present."

"Hmm. Good point." She folds her arms on my chest and sets her chin on them, studying me. "But I like to think that we would have gotten together anyway. That something this good...it's just meant to be, and nothing can stop it."

I sit on that concept for a moment. "You think we would have found our way to each other one way or another?"

She shrugs. "It's a nice thought."

"Yeah," I murmur, running my hand through her hair. "It is."

Whether it's the truth or not, I'm going to go with it. I'm

going to choose to believe that the good things in life are always searching for us, just as we're searching for them, and that something as special as what Hannah and I have really is meant to be.

And is that the case?

I really don't care. I'm happy with the belief, happy here on this island with this life—this woman and this family. There's nothing else I need, and you could call that destiny, but I don't mind what label is put on it.

Just so long as it's mine.

# Also by Lenna Phoenix

All books: https://www.lennaphoenix.com

SILENT JOURNEY series

We Can Forever

We Can Stay

We Can Do

We Can Believe

We Can Again

We Can Thrive

# About the Author

Lenna Phoenix knows just because you can't see an illness doesn't mean it's not there. She writes heartwarming small town (steamy!) romance novels that beautifully portray the journey of women finding love while living with chronic illness.

 facebook.com/lennaphoenix

 amazon.com/stores/Lenna-Phoenix/author/B0DBMVHCQY

 instagram.com/lenna.phoenix.books